# Sardinian Sunset

C. L Kraemer

Published by Rogue Phoenix Press, LLP
Copyright © 2019

ISBN: 978-1-62420-520-0

Credits
Cover Art: Designs by Ms G

## Author's Note

Sardinia is considered a state within the country of Italy. However, the primary language is Sardinian, with Italian being a close second. Only those communities hosting international tourists might have people who are English speakers. Much of the dialogue in this story is written in either Italian or English for the ease of the reader. My Italian is passable. My Sardinian—non-existent.

# Prologue

*USA Today, Feb. 1, 2018*
**Ollolai, Italy is selling homes for $1.25. That's cheaper than a cappuccino.**

Ollolai, a hillside town toward the center of Sardinia, a large Mediterranean island west of Italy, is offering crumbling dwellings for 1 euro (about $1.25) in an effort to boost the shrinking population of the mini-metropolis, which dates back thousands of years.

The catch? You have to spend about $25,000 to renovate the home you buy and do the work within three years. You can sell it after five years.

Over the past half-century, as reported in official figures, the town's population has declined from 2,250 to 1,300, leaving hundreds of abandoned homes.

According to Britain's *Independent* newspaper, Ollolai sits on the slopes of Monte San Basilio Magno, and is one of the few remaining Sardinian towns where a local martial art, S'Istrumpa, is still practiced. It also keeps up traditional artisan crafts such as the weaving of baskets.

# Chapter One

Keys winging through the air, accompanied by an exasperated, "I have HAD IT!" announced the arrival of Olivia Francesca Porcu Martin. The unintended target, a replica of an ancient, Italian, wine container, shattered into shards on the floor. "I always hated that vase."

Traffic on the way home from work had her wondering if the State Mental Hospital had freed all the patients with keys to new cars, releasing them on the unsuspecting public. Her briefcase thunked to the floor, and she dropped to the sofa. Toeing off her high heels, Olivia sighed as she lay her head on the back of the cushion. "What I wouldn't give to fly away to a quiet Greek island and disappear."

Working was a distraction, nothing more. Years of living in the fashion her friends referred to as, *monk-like*, she had invested her earnings wisely, wanting for very little in the way of material items. Why couldn't she fly away? She huffed. "Where would I go, and what would I do?"

Sitting on her laurels didn't appeal. Her finance degree opened the door to a world of fast and furious; leave your emotions in the lobby. Another wistful sigh escaped her lips. "Something will show up. Just a matter of time." Leaning forward, she snagged the remote from the coffee table and turned on the local news.

"In other news, today… On the island of Sardinia, the mayor of a small village in the mountains is offering approximately two hundred abandoned and crumbling homes for sale for… are you ready?" The newscaster peered into the camera lens and waited an appropriate length of time. "…one Euro. That's right, one Euro. There is a catch, however," he chuckled, "Isn't there always? The purchaser must sign an agreement to refurbish the home to a livable state. The mayor figures it will take $25,000 to $30,000, and the new owners have three years to reach that goal."

Olivia was on the edge of the couch cushion, waiting for more information.

"We'll be right back."

She groaned. "Of course."

When the broadcast came back live, the newscasters moved to another story without divulging the name of the town. She knew she had some research to complete as soon as possible. "Comfort first." Olivia struggled from the couch and traded her work clothes for jeans, t-shirt and tennis shoes. She snatched the laptop from its resting place on her dresser and walked to the sofa. Folding her legs beneath her as she flipped open the laptop, she powered it up. "If this story isn't a con, I'm outta here. If not…well, can't hurt to check it out." The sound of fingers maneuvering computer keys muted the rest of the news. Olivia leaned against the cushions, folding her arms. "I'll be. They're serious." She tapped through the photos, stopping when she'd located the place in which she was most interested.

Decades old stones tumbled into a courtyard. The layout shown suggested the previous owners had some wealth at one point. *I wonder what could have happened to make them move?* Olivia scanned the rest of the pictures and noted the number assigned to the property.

"Tomorrow, I'm taking a vacation day and doing as much research as I can. I believe I hear the call of Mediterranean sirens. No point in ignoring their songs."

# Chapter Two

Salvatore Lucchesia, current mayor of Ollolai, Sardinia, Italy stared at the pile of correspondence covering his desk. The center was full of envelopes containing letters and money. To the right was a pile of phone message forms needing answers.

"What the heck have I done to myself?"

A dark head peeked around the corner of the open office door. "*Un attimo?*"

"*Si.* What do you need, Angelica?"

Angelica Porcu was the receptionist/secretary/office manager of the small city office. Nothing in the town of Ollolai happened without her knowledge.

"We have someone holding on the phone who wishes to speak with you."

Salvatore sighed. "Right now, it seems the whole world wants to speak to me. Why is this person any different?"

"You know the house at the end of SP29?"

"The old Porcu place, *si.*"

"Well, Olivia Francesca Porcu Martin is on the phone and interested in buying it."

Sal's eyes widened. The story of the Porcu family at the end of SP29 was a tale spun right out of the movies in Rome.

"Francesca Porcu?"

"Olivia Francesca Porcu Martin. Please, Sal, she's calling from America."

"Okay, but no one else. I need time to sort these requests out."

Angelica scurried to her desk. "Hello? Thank you for waiting, Signorina Martin. I will connect you with *il sindaco* now." Angelica pushed the connect button and heard the telephone in the mayor's office ring. *Just a matter of time now.*

~ * ~

Olivia spent most of the evening researching Sardinia and the surrounding islands. She knew her heritage included Italian, as her grandmother spoke the language to her during childhood. In fact, when she started school at five, her mother, Anya Martin, was quite irritated at having to reteach her daughter English. It was the incident that pushed her to restrict Olivia's visits to her Nonna.

Pictures of the island pulled at Olivia's sense of adventure. She was not tethered to the Northwest. Her one act of rebelliousness was to leave New York and move to the West Coast for college. The move proved prophetic for her life. Graduating summa cum laude from Stanford, Olivia accepted a position with a financial agency in Portland, Oregon. Her professional life was a roaring success. The only fly in the ointment was when she'd tried a relationship once and still smarted from the fallout. *Nope. Not for me.* Why shouldn't she move to Sardinia? She'd wisely invested funds set aside from her checks and didn't need to work. A villa, albeit small, on an Italian island in the Mediterranean? What was not to like?

Livy set her sights on the two-story building. She quickly figured the time difference and set her alarm to call as early in their morning as she could. By the end of this week, she was going to be the proud owner of a home in Sardinia. She could only hope it wasn't just a pile of rocks.

The following day, Olivia made the call to the Mayor's office in Ollolai. It was listed as the contact point. She spoke with a very nice lady who put her through to the man himself.

"This is Salvatore Lucchesia. To whom am I speaking?"

Livy had to stifle a giggle. He was not comfortable speaking English as was evident by his stilted, proper use. She figured she would try her Italian, as rusty as it was, and see how far she could get. "Yes, Mr. Mayor. I hope you will bear with my feeble attempts at Italian."

"That's not Italian."

*Oh, no. Here it comes.*

"You are speaking Sardinian. If I had any doubt as to your identity, this has wiped away all my hesitations."

"Sardinian? But, how…?" Livy was confused.

"You must have a family member who was Sardinian." the mayor commented.

"I'm not sure about Sardinian, but my Nonna said she was Italian. She's the one who taught me to speak this language."

Salvatore knew the tale of the lost love was true. "I must say, you do the language proud. How might I be of assistance?"

Livy barreled forward. "I'm very interested in the property you list at the end of SP29. I'd like to put a bid on it."

"Okay. You do understand you must sign paperwork that obligates you to make the property livable within three years? After that time, if you wish to sell, you may, but we will need an affidavit stating your intentions."

Olivia smiled. "Of course, sir. I have no intention of selling should I get this property. I'm moving and staying. I was under the impression that was your purpose in selling these homes."

"Si. We welcome new people to our community and hope they will bring or start families here. I believe you have the attitude we want in Ollolai. Once I have the signed paperwork, and receive your one Euro, I'll take the picture from our website."

"Great. Please send the paperwork to my fax number, 1-503-222-4141. I'll sign it, fax it back, and send a payment to the bank. I'll need to set up an account if I'm going to live there, anyway. Will that work?"

Salvatore finished writing the number on his notepad. "Yes. The paperwork will be in Italian. Do you have resources to have it translated?"

"I'll find a way. Thank you for your time. I hope we meet soon.

*Ciao.*"

"*Ciao*, Signorina Porcu Martin."

The fax machine Olivia used as part of her computer started beeping and spitting out paper. *They are fast. I just hope everything else will go as quickly.*

# Chapter Three

Olivia tucked the last personal item into her briefcase and snapped the lid shut. *There.* There was little to indicate this office belonged to anyone.

"Olivia?" Taylor poked her head in the doorway. "Where are your personal things? Pictures, plants, all the little do-dads you used to have here?"

Olivia thought about lying but why? Taylor was a friend, a good one at that, and she deserved to know the truth. "My last day is Friday."

"What? Where are you going? Did you finally start the company you were planning?"

Livy put up a hand to stop the deluge of questions. "First…no, I didn't start a company—yet. Second, I'm leaving the country and moving to Sardinia."

Taylor, her mouth slightly opened, stood, disbelief on her face. "I guess congratulations are in order."

Livy could see Tay was struggling to wrap her mind around something. "Tay? What's the problem?"

Tears threated to cascade down Tay's cheeks. "What am I going to do? You're the only one who has even a small clue as to what I'm dealing with; the only one I trust enough to tell the truth to. If you move to another country, I'll have no one!"

Olivia looked at the waterlogged eyes. "Taylor? It's the 21$^{st}$ century. We can email, text or call each other. Distance can't break our friendship. You will always have a place to stay, or live if you want. I've seen the pictures of the place I've bought…"

Taylor's eyes widened. "Bought?"

"Yes, bought. Anyway, there is enough room for plenty of guests." Livy's face brightened. "A bed and breakfast. Yes!"

"Bed and breakfast?"

Livy sat at the computer and pulled up the pictures of the home she owned in Ollolai. "See? Plenty of room." She smiled.

Taylor lifted a brow. "Sure, if you're into camping. What in the world have you done?"

Olivia leaned against the back of her chair. She waved her hand at the seat opposite. "Have a sit down. This is going to take more than five minutes."

Tay sat and waited for the story to begin.

"It's been about a month now since I started down this path…"

Half an hour later, Taylor had all the details of Olivia's new adventure. "What I would give to be able to go with you."

"The invitation is always open. You can stay a day, a year or to the end of your life. I'd love to have you close. But I know you have an agenda of your own. I hope it works to your favor."

"I've taken steps to start the process. We'll see how well the system in place works."

# Chapter Four

Clusters of thoughts crowded Olivia's brain clouding her insight to the hovering presence to her right. When she tried to move that direction, a wall of humanity stopped her motion. Returning to her situation of the moment, she turned to stare at the impediment. "Excuse me?"

She stared at a face she'd not seen in several months. "Brian. How?"

"Were you really going to leave town without telling me?" His blue eyes appeared so earnest she almost believed him. Then she remembered to whom she spoke.

"I was under the distinct impression you didn't care and, frankly, I don't give a damn whether you know or not. You closed the door on—us—several months ago."

"Wow. You're going all *Gone with the Wind* on me. I've come to my senses and thought maybe…"

"Don't think. Don't what if, if only, or all the things you suspect will work to sway me right this moment." She pushed past him. "I'm leaving the Northwest. Goodbye, Brian." Olivia bolted to the gate for the pre-flight security dance. *If that jerk made me miss my plane, I swear, I'll kill him.* She arrived at the waiting area noting she had twenty minutes to spare. After checking in with the airline personnel, she sat watching the tarmac and planes ferry people in and out of the Portland airport. There were things she'd miss about Oregon, but Brian Froeschner was not one of them.

The only time she'd taken down her self-imposed, emotional wall, the guy turned out to be a philandering letch. She'd tired of feeling as though she were an observer in her own life. His ministrations to con her into thinking he was interested in her while he was trying to mine her for financial, i.e. insider information, to plump his portfolio wore her out. Early in the relationship after yet another lunch spent pretending he wasn't ogling every female in the place, Olivia decided to end the charade.

"Brian, I think we need to end this, this whatever it is, we have. You aren't interested in me, and it's painfully obvious to everyone in the room; including me. Don't call again."

She got up and left him, mouth gaping. Stepping into the mist of a winter's day, Livy reveled in the sensation of sunshine. She hadn't realized the weight of the deception he was attempting to pull off was so heavy. She smiled at a passerby and hummed all the way back to the office, pulling his file, and trading portfolios with Liam, a burly Rugby player and fellow broker, for a sedate, retired couple only interested in *safe* stocks.

He swept into her office around two the same afternoon, bearing a single red rose and the specialty coffee she liked so well. Accepting the coffee, she directed him down the hall, commenting that Liam would love the rose. Later, Liam would ask why she was willing to give up such a lucrative client. Her mumbled comment spoke to downsizing her risk factors. She asked him to inform her when the client was to be in the office for a conference. It was pure coincidence her outside appointments seemed to coincide with these visits.

Livy sighed. "And that's why I have no use for romance or men in my life."

When her flight was announced over the speaker, Olivia Martin stoically marched down the boarding corridor to one of the planes flying her *home*. Taking her seat in business class, she tucked her purse beneath her feet, having stowed her carryon overhead. She allowed the muscles of her neck to loosen.

"Ma'am?" The attendant gently touched her arm. "You need to bring your seat back fully upright and buckle up. Once we reach altitude, the lights will go off and you can relax."

There was a sudden kerfluffle at the entry door. The voice of an excited female was speaking rapidly, met by a response, presumably from the attendant, which seemed to calm the late passenger. The routine for departure from PDX continued, albeit a few minutes late.

*Now what?* Olivia felt annoyance starting to build behind her eyes. *Just chill. You have all the time in the world.* When the attendant escorted the person toward Olivia's row, she cringed and turned her gaze to outside the window. The last thing she needed on a long flight was some over-apologetic person babbling away.

The soul sat next to her, placing an item beneath the seat, and buckled in as instructed. Olivia continued to stare at the scenery until she heard the engines ramp up. A bumping motion let the passengers know they were rolling away from the terminal. She watched rainbows created by moments of sunshine through summer showers. Her departure was bittersweet. Portland had been good to her, but the time had arrived for Olivia Francesca Porcu Martin to start living. Imagining sunshine and the dulcet sounds of oak trees whispering in warm Mediterranean breezes helped her settle for the flight to a new life.

"Is the invitation to stay at your new home still open?" The familiar voice jolted Livy from her reverie.

"Tay! You made it!"

"I thought about it and decided there was no time like the present to get myself together. I hope you meant what you said about me staying with you."

"Of course, but right now, the place is in dire need of repairs. You're welcome to share my hotel while I work to make a part of the house livable."

"I may take you up on that if they don't have any rooms open. In the meantime, I think we might consider napping a bit. It's going to be a long few flights."

Olivia and Taylor waited until the seat belt sign was turned off. They swapped ideas on the future of Livy's new home and giggled with excitement over their adventure. When they stretched out their seats, both quickly dropped into a light slumber.

~ * ~

The flights were uneventful, thankfully, and Olivia was glad Taylor decided to accompany her on this journey. Customs, luggage, and car rental moved along without a hitch. Tay opted to rent a vehicle for herself to explore on her own while Olivia was dealing with the business of hiring a construction company to begin repairs on her home. Driving along the west coast of the island from Alghero Airport toward her destination, Olivia observed the landscape change from commercial tourist to local inhabitant. The more local-inhabitant towns and farms she witnessed, the more she felt her body relax. This was better than she hoped. She opted to turn off the air conditioning and roll down the car window to experience the island in all its glory.

Salt air and petrol fumes were replaced by the aroma of green; green fields of hay, grapes for wine, and vegetables. The animal farms provided their own essence depending on the livestock. She continued to check the rearview mirror, keeping Taylor's little Fiat in her sights, when she realized her driving speed had slowed compared to her habit in the States. Why not? She wasn't in a hurry to get anywhere fast. Turning into the driveway of the inn where she was staying until the home was finished, Olivia parked her rented vehicle then checked in.

Taylor parked next to Olivia and followed her into the reception area. She was in luck. There was a room available two doors down from Olivia's. Taylor paid for a week in advance. She'd decide at that time if she were going to stay longer.

The pair grabbed their keys and headed in the direction of their rooms.

"Meet me in the bar for a glass of wine?" Olivia stopped at her door.

"Half an hour?" Taylor set her suitcase on the sidewalk.

"Sounds good to me. I'll see you there." Olivia opened her door, and situating her belongings, changed to a comfortable pair of jeans, t-shirt, and sandals. Realizing the half hour was nearly up, she stepped outside her room and waited for Taylor.

The pair meandered to the small restaurant and ordered glasses of the local alcoholic delicacy, slipping to the outside patio to enjoy the evening. The air whispered of new beginnings. Warblers darted around the sky chatting and bringing a happy end to a long journey.

*I've come home.* Olivia sighed and took a sip of the local wine. The fear she'd carried since making this decision evaporated into the cooling night air. She looked at her friend. "Tomorrow, Ollolai."

Taylor took a sip of the wine and allowed the liquid to soothe her soul. "Yes."

# Chapter Five

The day dawned with an azure sky teasing voluminous white clouds from the horizon. Olivia opened the drapes to take in the view. She wanted to smell the air and feel sun on her face, so she opted to have her breakfast on the restaurant's veranda. The service was quick, and the hotel guests appeared caught up in plans to explore the island, leaving her to her thoughts. She'd opted to allow Taylor to sleep this morning and would check on her before leaving. After all, this was her home and her journey of discovery. Taylor was here to relax and try to recover from the situation back in Portland.

"Thanks for not waking me up, friend." Taylor sat at the table.

"I thought you might enjoy exploring a little. After all, this house stuff is my thing and, from what I hear around me, there is a lot to do on this island."

Taylor chuckled. "I won't do anything until I get some coffee." Magically, a full cup of coffee appeared before her. She looked up into a pair of dark brown eyes smiling her direction.

"*Buon giorno, signorina.*" He whisked away only to return with a menu. "When you are ready." And off he went.

"Wow. They are amazing here." Taylor scanned the items and made her decision. As the menu touched the table, the waiter was at her elbow.

"What may I bring you?" His eyes twinkled and a warm smile lit up his face.

Taylor ordered her meal and sat drinking her coffee. "Livy?"

"Hmm?"

"I think I'd like to go to the beach and walk on the sand, maybe do a bit of sailing. The wind on my cheeks and sun in my eyes will help clear my head. I hope you don't mind."

"No. Just make sure you take your phone. That way if anything happens you can contact me. Okay? Safety, girlfriend, safety."

"You got it." Taylor's food arrived and silence descended on the table as the pair were lost in their thoughts.

When they finished, paid the bill and headed back to their rooms, the girls ran over the schedules they hoped to keep on this day, promising to check in often. They hugged and headed their separate directions.

Olivia had only one discovery in mind—her home. After checking at the front desk to verify the route into Ollolai, she started the journey to her new incarnation. She was in no hurry to arrive at the town center, but the trip was less than a mile from her hotel. She cruised the narrow streets at a respectful speed and, quickly, located a parking spot at the town square.

Strolling along the avenue, she passed a couple restaurants emitting the most enticing aromas. Somewhere close by was a bakery. The fragrance of freshly baked bread was making her mouth water. *Living here could be dangerous to my waistline. Maybe it's best that I don't cook.* She checked her map, noting the *Uficio Postale*, post office, and realizing the city hall was a few steps away.

She entered city hall. The building, while new-ish, still smelled of history and stories yet to be told.

"*Si. Come posso aiutarvi?*"

"*Parli iglesi?*"

"A little." The dark-haired woman behind the desk leaned back in her chair. "What do you wish?"

"My name is Olivia Francesca Porcu Martin. I believe there are some papers I still need to sign to get my home? And I need directions."

"*Oh, si, si. Un atimo.*"

The woman left the room, returning with a manila file folder and a pen. She put the folder on the desk and motioned to Olivia to have a seat. "I will need you to sign, here," she pointed to a spot on the official document, "and here. Then I will provide you the keys to your home and a map."

Livy looked at the document. "May I have a copy?"

"*Naturalmente.*"

She signed in the spots indicated and put the pen on the desk. "I don't know why I'm being so OCD." The woman stifled a giggle. "I mean, I'm not planning on going anywhere and everyone will know where I live. *Siamo spiacenti.*"

"My name is Angelica Porcu. We are distant cousins, so, *si*, I will know where you live. Allow me to make a copy for you. I'll bring it back along with the key and address of your home. I can give you clear directions to get there. Any other *informazioni* you require I'll be able to provide if you call."

Angelica returned with a manila envelope bulging with documents and a very old iron key, then walked Olivia to the sidewalk. She pointed west and provided Olivia with detailed instructions on how to travel the quarter mile to her home.

Olivia turned to her distant cousin. "*Grazie.*"

"Welcome home, Olivia Porcu."

Livy waved and, wearing a large grin, went back to her vehicle to find her home. The directions she'd been given were spot on. She realized once she drove up the earthen driveway that walking might have been faster. A nervous giggle escaped her. All her worries evaporated the moment she set eyes on the home. It was not a mansion but not a ruin, either. The walls still stood and, apparently, the doors and windows were intact, but all she could see was the front of the building and property. The lot butted up to a small hill at the end of SP29. Far enough from town to be private but close enough to walk, if necessary. From the looks of the surrounding area, she would probably be able to get cell service.

"Olivia Francesca Porcu Martin, get your butt out of this vehicle and inspect the area, you ninny. You can speculate until your brain blows up. Feet on the ground will verify what and how much needs work."

She got out of the car and walked to the front of the building. She noted that, unlike most of the homes in town, this house sported a porch on the front. *Unusual.* The other buildings in town abutted the narrow lanes. She only noticed balconies on the second floors which made sense if you took into consideration the front of the home was right on the busy street. Olivia tried the door and felt chagrined when it was locked. She pulled out the key she'd been given and used it.

"Surprise! It works." A quick survey of the rooms before her showed a simple layout. Immediately in front of her was the area she presumed to be the living room. A stone fireplace took up one wall. The rocks were local and probably had been taken from the very lot where the house was built. At one time, the interior had been whitewashed, but time and neglect left everything in a layer of fine dust. She could see where pictures had been placed on the walls and there were still a few tattered rugs on the floor beneath a layer of dirt. Scuff marks indicated furnishings had been sparse. When she thought on it, the last inhabitant of this place had been here until about 1955; nearly three quarters of a century ago.

A double doorway opened into the kitchen and dining area. Unlike the states, there were no built-in cupboards. However, a hand carved hutch was pushed against the wall. She could see where the pots had been hanging near a wood stove—a real stove using wood for cooking and heat. *Well there's the first expense.* About three feet to the left of the stove stood a square box with two handles. *Oh, a small cupboard.* She opened one of the doors. "I don't believe it. A refrigerator. Good lord, it must be nearly a hundred years old. I wonder if it works."

Only time and better wiring would tell. Livy found a staircase at the end of one wall in the kitchen and took it to the second floor. She drifted through bedrooms, one bathroom, and a water closet, taking pictures on her phone for reference. *That's going to have to change. Especially if I want to have a B & B.* She took in plumbing done in the twenties and thirties as well as wiring of about the same era. Everywhere she looked the euros added up. *Oh, well. I couldn't buy a modular back in the states for what it will cost to get this place into living order.* She descended the stairs and walked to the counter. Over the large sink was a window. Surprisingly, the glass was still in place. Livy peered into the back area noting a three-sided wooden shed. She was only guessing but thought the family might have had sheep, chickens or, in this area, donkeys. After all, Sardinians, her people, were very self-sufficient. They'd lived on the island since the Neolithic age. With all the pictures she needed of each room, Olivia left the house, locking the front door, and stood on the porch gazing at the surrounding hills. The scent of Mediterranean scrub brush and a hint of oak filtered by on the breeze.

"I need to eat. I'm starved. I haven't heard from Taylor yet. That worries me. I hope she just lost track of time… Maybe, I'll call after I order dinner to see where she is." She took the few steps off the portico and got into her rental. A garage was going to be a necessity too. What she thought was a garage had been nothing more than a storage shed off the kitchen. *Phew. More money.* Starting the engine, Olivia put the car in gear and headed back to her current lodgings.

"I only hope it doesn't take three years to finish the job."

# Chapter Six

Olivia tapped a finger on the windowsill. "Come on, Taylor, pick up the phone. Where the hell *are* you?" She'd dialed the number from her table at dinner, but the call went to voice mail. She was trying again this morning. If she didn't get any answer, her next stop before going to her house would be the mayor's office in Ollolai to make a missing person's report. Okay, maybe she was overreacting, but Taylor was her friend. News reports from the last couple years weren't encouraging for single American women in foreign countries.

This was unlike her. A quick trip to the front desk to ask them to do a welfare check had proven her clothing was just the way it had been when she left yesterday. The bed had not been slept in.

Livy's stomach soured. "Oh, god! What have I done to my friend?"

She drove directly to the town center and the mayor's office. She opened the door to the office, finding Angelica at her desk.

"Good morning, cousin. What can I do for you today?" Angelica smiled.

Olivia wrung her hands. "My friend, Taylor Maxwell, decided to take a vacation here. I offered her a place to stay, and she took the offer. Yesterday, when I first came here, she opted to do some sightseeing while I checked out the house. I haven't seen her since around nine in the morning when we went our separate ways." Olivia put up a hand before Angelica could say anything. "She is not the type of person to go off with some handsome lothario and party the night away. She is engaged and waiting for her fiancé to return from—the war zone. I'm very worried. What do I need to do to file a missing person report?"

Angelica thought and pulled open a drawer. "Let's start here with this paperwork. I'll do some investigating and contact the American consulate. Just leave your number with me, and we'll do all we can to try to find your friend." She hesitated for a moment. "It's what families do for each other; even, distant cousins."

They sat and completed a mountain of paperwork with Olivia filling in as much information as she could remember. When she walked out of the mayor's office two hours later, her stomach hurt as well as her heart. At this point, she needed to stay positive.

# Chapter Seven

Lightning slashed across the sky and thunder drummed in Destiny's ears. The strange vessel began to turn on its axis, swirling faster with each passing second. Destiny lost her balance. Her head hit the floor hard. She heard the crack then nothing more except roaring in her ears.

When she opened her eyes, sunshine filled the tiny cabin. She pressed her hands to her temples trying to ease the pain throbbing through her head. Slowly, she found her way to the deck.

The sky was a vivid blue with a few clouds lying close to the horizon, Reid's ship was nowhere to be seen, although the sailboat sat in the same cove. She didn't know how to sail a boat; didn't have any idea how to get to land. Would Reid sail without her? Good Lord, she hoped not. She'd have to find another job, and she'd have to find another man she could trust.

A boat passed by, and she waved at it, hoping someone would rescue her. It came about and headed back her direction. Watching the craft come closer, she held her breath, praying for her safety.

"Can we help?" someone from the vessel asked as it pulled up close. "You look stranded."

"I'm lost. Yes, stranded," Destiny admitted, shrugging her shoulders as she tried to assess this man who seemed to be offering aid. "Can you take me somewhere close by?" While she'd made several trips with Captain Stewart, she'd never been on the land, never left the boat. She had no idea what this island had to offer.

"Where are we?"

"Sardinia. I'll take you to Ollolai. That's where I'm staying. You know anybody there?"

"No," she was shaking her head and wondering what she would do to survive. "I can cook. Does anyone need a cook?"

The man chuckled. "I've heard another guest at the hotel mentioning her need. Climb aboard."

~ * ~

Destiny Rose groaned. "Where the hell am I?" Her head pounded and, she surmised, she must have hit it on one of the many rocks covering the interior of this—what the hell was this anyway? She must be in a newer century than the last. Her head throbbed, and she placed a hand on the back, flinching at the pain. Oh, right. Boat, water, storm, floor. And a rescuer, not a pirate, assisting her to the shore. How the heck did she get from the coast to this, thing?

She could only bide her time, of which she had plenty, to discover her final destination. A jet keened overhead giving her the hope this was the 20$^{th}$ century. *Well, of course it must be, you silly goose. You were brought to the center of town in a motorized vehicle. I must have walked here. But why?* She tested her limbs by stretching; waiting for the inevitable pain of something broken and was pleased to find her parts in good working order. She sat up and observed the three-sided structure. "Hmmm. Manger? Could have been much worse. I've a covered refuge, for now. This will give me time to explore where the fates have landed me."

Cloaking herself in a cover of wariness, she peeked around the corner of the stone shed. The small out-building was placed at the back of a home two-stories in size and encompassing some area. She noted a path leading around the side. If the shed where she currently stood was a home for animals, they'd been gone for a long time. No fresh hay or *presents* littered the rocky ground. She listened carefully but detected little movement in the surrounding hills. *The area is not heavily peopled.*

A movement caught her attention. She noted a face appear in one of the windows on the ground floor. Destiny pulled back into the shed. She stilled her pounding heartbeat, afraid the soul inside the building would hear and chase her away. *Don't be such a dunce.* Subterfuge was not her strong point. *Doesn't need to be.* Standing against the back wall, she was sweating profusely. Her 19th century clothing was hot, scratchy and, with the help of a gentle breeze, alerted her to the smell of brine and oily cooking clinging to her person. *Fates be cursed, I need a bath.* An abode with four walls and water close by would be deeply welcomed. There may not be creatures seeking her for a midnight dinner, but she wasn't about to tempt the fates any more than necessary.

A motorized sound reached her ears followed by crunching fading into the distance. Hope she might explore the bigger structure blossomed. A familiar tickle spread across her scalp. This had to be her new assignment. Destiny scratched her head then stepped into the open. No sounds assaulted her ears. The person inside the structure must have left. Marks about the size of a supply wagon showed a vehicle moving toward a faint line down the hill, which must be a road.

She inched her way across the back of the house checking each point of entry. Window—no, unable to open. Second window—same result. Bloody hell, was she going to have to stay in that little…place tonight? Not the optimal choice. She sighed and pulled up tall. One more window. Pulling on the bottom of the frame resulted in movement. The squeal of swollen wood on swollen wood caused her ears to ache. In one quick movement, she pulled up, swung over the frame and landed on smooth stones.

Sliding down the sturdy wall, she blew out a breath. Allowing the span of a few minutes to pass in which she steadied her pounding heart, Destiny stood and closed the window. Pulling *in* the frame didn't seem to have the same effect. No screeching. *Now to do a quick surveillance of the property.* She poked her head into an area she presumed to be the sitting room. Down a long hallway to a sleeping room on the first floor complete with a bathing room. *Thank goodness.*

She peered around for a bucket to fill the white horse trough she thought must be for said purpose. There were some fancy knobs on one side. Her curiosity pushed her to twist them. Nothing. *Well, what are they for then?* There must be a well close by. Opposite the horse trough was a funny looking chair. Destiny was puzzled by this bit of furniture. It didn't face a mirror but the trough. *Why would people wish to place a chair in that spot? Bugger.* There was so much catching up she needed to do before the end of the week. The sands of time were slipping through her fingers. She had the sensation this task wasn't meant to be but a brief interlude into the life of the assigned.

She poked around some of the other rooms on the first floor. A quick jaunt up the stairs and a brief inventory of the remaining rooms, including another bathing room with the same weird set up of funny chair facing a horse trough. *Why would people bring their horses up to the second floor and watch them drink? Were they that valuable?* All the exploration in a house covered in decades of dust and dirt was taking its toll on Destiny. Trudging down the stairs to the first floor, she decided if she was going to stay here for the night, it might prove to her advantage to stay near the ground. Recovery would be easier with bumps and bruises as opposed to broken bones should she need to leave in a hurry. Traveling back to the kitchen, she spotted a narrow door at one end of the room. Opening the closure proved to expose storage for cleaning equipment. Thank goodness the broom appeared to be the same, whatever time this was. She grabbed the tool and determined she'd pick one of the rooms and give it a dust up.

The chamber, second opening off the hallway, was her choice for tonight's slumber. She couldn't recall peering inside this door. The window beckoned. She jimmied it open to allow fresh, cool air to enter and escort some of the dust motes to the exterior of the house. Using skills she'd been called upon to employ at her last location, Destiny dry-swabbed the floor with the broom. The center of the room was covered with a patterned carpet. Once she shuttled the dirt into the hall, she turned to view her chosen sleeping chamber. The sun shone on a carpet of such quality Destiny gasped. She dropped to her knees, ignoring the fine dust marking her dark britches. Gently, reverently, she reached out her hand and caressed the quality fabric. The weaving was the finest she could recall seeing—ever. Much as she hated to admit it, the finished product rivaled her own. This night she would experience the pride of Sardinia. Maybe a good night's rest might help her come up with a plan to help this assignment—person. She really was going to have to speak to the boss about a vacation. Too many assignments in too short of a time were dulling her ability to relate to them as people.

Twinges slicing through her forehead drew a moan from the traveler. "Not now. I don't have time for this." The warning was a precursor to a raging headache rivaling a drunk's hangover. It was her recompense for time travel. *Bed. Sleep will chase away the demon.* Destiny lay on the magnificent carpet and easily slid into a deep slumber.

# Chapter Eight

A night of rest knowing there was a roof over your head and enough barriers to discourage an attacker helped Destiny's plan drop into place. Upon opening her eyes in the morning, she noticed a rucksack next to her makeshift bed. She opened the bag to find a treasure trove of items to assist her with this assignment. A small blue booklet with a fair resemblance to herself sported several official seals from different locations about the globe. A booklet with papers held together by a curved wire had a title of *Research* handprinted on the front. Once she opened the cover, she read a few lines and realized the information was about the Nuragic structures of settlers living in the area three thousand years ago and still standing today. In writing visible only to her dream weaver eyes, she noted her cover story was she was a student studying the ruins for a degree in Archeology, specifically ancient weaving.

The last items placed in her bag appeared to be clothing of the current era. Items she recognized her rescuer wearing. An instruction sheet was included giving her the accepted way to wear the articles. She quickly stripped out of her 19th century wear and into the new clothes. She quite liked the pants; they were comfortable, sturdy, and covered her entire legs. The shoes were a tad confusing, but once she mastered the short stockings, she realized these foot coverings were going to provide her more flexibility than the oversized boots she'd grown accustomed to wearing. Rays of warm sunlight brightened the room.

Destiny hastened her movement. She quickly repacked the rucksack and made her way to the kitchen area. Lifting and pushing out the window, she peered out as far as possible to ascertain if others were close by. A relieved sigh slipped past her lips on discovering she was alone. The rucksack dropped to the ground followed by her body. She closed the window and scooted along the side of the house to the front corner. Her plan was to wait on the front steps until the owner returned. She was certain once she spotted the assignment—owner—what she was to do would be obvious. Covertly she made her way to the steps of the home, pulling out her booklet to read the material within the covers. Best to know what she was supposed to be studying.

The crunch of vehicle wheels coming up the drive alerted her to the arrival of her latest dreamer. She faced a 20th century vehicle similar to the one driven by her rescuer. *Thank goodness. Maybe, they'll be able to find where to pump the water.* She was in sore need of bathing. The vehicle slowed; the occupant not exiting nor turning off the motor. Destiny resisted the urge to look up wondering why the driver hesitated. She concentrated on the book but opted to change her tactic. Looking up, she smiled. The simple act seemed to work. She heard the click and watched as the door opened and the driver exited. The young female approached Destiny.

"Can I help you?"

*Not British or Sardinian. Maybe American?* "Morning, Miss. The lady at the mayor's office said I might be able to find temporary work and, maybe, lodging here."

Olivia allowed a frown to cover her face. She wasn't accustomed to people knowing her business. *Hold it. Small town. Everyone knows everyone else's business. Get used to it or go back to the states.* "What are you looking to do?"

"Whatever needs doing, Miss. I've picked up a great many skills on my travels."

"You're British?"

"Yes, ma'am. I'm taking a year sabbatical from Oxford to get in some field study to do research for my Masters' thesis on ancient civilizations. One of the oldest civilizations was from this particular area of the Mediterranean."

"Really? I didn't know." Olivia was warming to this brave traveler. "I'm afraid I haven't much work in the way of housekeeping or the like. I'm sure you can see my residence is in dire need of repair. Maybe the hotel where I'm staying will have an opening."

Destiny could feel the situation slipping from her control. "Beg pardon, Miss?"

"Oh, sorry. Olivia Martin."

"Destiny Rose."

"What a beautiful name."

"Thank you. Will you be making repairs to your home?"

Olivia puffed out a breath. "Yes, but I'm feeling a bit overwhelmed. While I have a reasonably long amount of time to complete the repairs, I want to live in my home as soon as possible. It will save money that I can invest back into my house. I just don't know where to start."

Destiny knew she had to tread lightly here. "What if I act as a watch guard? You can feel certain your home will be protected, and I'll be able to study without worrying about my budget being broken. Inns are nice but can be very noisy if one wants to concentrate. I can swing a hammer with the best of them. I would just need some floor space to sleep and study. I'm capable of cooking my own meals."

Olivia's eyes lit up. "You cook?"

"Fairly well, if I say so myself."

Livy worried her bottom lip. "Okay. But if I feel the least bit threatened or sense things are not as they should be, I have no problem calling the *Polizi* to come haul you away and lock you up."

Destiny slowly released a breath she'd been holding. "As my Aussie roommate at Oxford would say, fair dinkum."

The two shook hands. Destiny followed Olivia through the front door. Something about the young lady tugged at Destiny's memory. Maybe it was her voice or the hazel eyes, she wasn't sure. She knew, eventually, whatever was triggering her memory would come forward.

Olivia stopped suddenly, only moving when Destiny bumped into her. "Someone has been in the house." There was no question; it was a statement full of consternation and concern.

Destiny ventured to ask. "How can you tell?"

Livy turned toward Destiny and slowly raised a brow. "The air in this room doesn't smell sixty years old. Someone has come in and aired out the place or *Le Janas* [faeries] have invaded my home thinking it completely abandoned." She crossed her arms, eyes narrowing.

Destiny swallowed hard. "I, uh, I, uh, oh, bloody hell. It was me. I found a way through the kitchen window and stayed in one of the ground floor rooms. I wanted to find a way to thank the owner."

Olivia continued to stare at Destiny, letting her squirm beneath her glare. "Thank you. Don't you have any lodging set up?"

Panic crawled up Destiny's throat. She had the good sense to blush. "I'm studying the Nuragic ruins in the area and got so caught up in the amazing architecture, I lost track of time. Sunset was quickly darkening the area, and this was the closest dwelling. I didn't wish to sleep in the donkey shed for fear of wild animals. I'm really sorry." She lowered her eyes and affected a sorrowful expression.

Olivia wasn't sure if she wanted to believe this young student or not. She'd been honest enough to wait out front but neglected to mention her stay the previous night. "As I said, if I don't feel comfortable or suspect any felonious actions on your part, I've no hesitation to do what is necessary to keep my home and myself safe. Are we clear?"

"Yes."

"Good. Do you want to stay at the house while you complete your research?"

"If you will allow me to."

"Yes. A presence in the home might deter unwanted visitors of the two-legged and four-legged kind. As far as the crawly, slithery type? You're on your own."

"Thanks."

Olivia pulled a notebook from her bag along with a tape measure. "Destiny? May I ask you to help me get measurements?"

"Of course." She placed her rucksack on the floor in the kitchen area.

Livy sniffed the air and wrinkled her nose. "It smells like dead fish in here. That odor wasn't here yesterday. I would've remembered."

Destiny straightened up. "I'm sorry. It must be my clothing. I've been so busy researching and writing, I've reverted to an older era for cleaning. I find the nearest natural water and go in with all my clothing on. The last time was on one of the local beaches. I didn't realize it would smell."

"Uhm, okay." Olivia found the idea very strange. Her schooling had been in Finance, not Archeology involving field work. "When we finish here, we can take your stuff to the local laundromat and give it a good cleaning."

Panic flooded Destiny's chest. Her 19th century clothing would not hold up well to the modern-day cleaners. "As you wish. You're the boss."

"Lord, *please*. Don't call me that. I'm just Olivia or Livy."

"Of course."

For the next hour and a half, the two women measured all the windows, floor space, and pretty much anything not moving fast enough. When Olivia mentioned burning the carpet from the room where Destiny spent the night, she turned, horror showing on her face.

"Please don't do that. Allow me to do my best to clean it. Sardinian carpets are rated in the same class as Persian carpets."

Livy looked skeptical. "Right…"

Destiny cleared her throat. "You have found me out."

Olivia waited.

"My bachelor's is in Archeology. I'm researching my master's in ancient textiles, weaving specifically."

"You weave?"

"Uhm, yes. Why?"

Livy's face lit up. "I have something to show you." She bustled down the hallway to beneath the stairs, waiting for the college student to follow. Once Destiny arrived next to Livy, she opened a door built seamlessly into the stairwell, exposing descending steps. Her last visit had revealed this entry. She'd leaned against what she thought was solid, only to experience a cool breeze tickling her ankles. A gentle push on the wall, and the hidden door opened. Venturing as far as the light would allow, she glimpsed the large item languishing in the corner venturing a guess as to the item's purpose. Turning on a torch, Destiny couldn't remember her having, Livy gingerly took the steps to the bottom. She shined the light around a stone walled cellar, stopping on a large item in the corner wearing a cloak of spider webs and years of dust. "Is this what I think?"

Destiny felt the flush of her skin from head to toes. She walked to the wooden loom and touched one side. The machine was made from the local oak trees and expertly carved. Even with the dust of decades, the parts glowed with warmth. The shuttle hung from a post. She ventured closer to look at the surface worn smooth by the diligent hands of many weavers.

"This is a magnificent work of art. Do you know how to weave?" She turned to face Olivia.

Livy shook her head. "I'm afraid that skill died when my grandmother left Italy."

A tug of memory struck the weaver. *That's it. This is the completing of this family's circle.* She realized she'd been here previously. She was the weaver who'd fulfilled the wish of a young Sardinian girl to leave an island steeped in sorrow. She turned and grasped the fine wood. Memories roared at her, overwhelming and filling in the gaps.

Olivia watched as Destiny's eyes rolled back in her head. She emitted a groan and slumped to the ground. Olivia panicked. *What now?* She sprinted across the room, leaning down to feel for a pulse. The girl's skin was clammy and cool to the touch. *I wonder when was the last time she ate?*

"What happened?"

Olivia jumped then offered a hand to Destiny, allowing her to sit. "I don't know. You touched the loom, groaned, and, well, passed out. Have you eaten lately?"

"I don't recall. Blimey, but my head is swimming."

The women cautiously raised from the cool floor.

"I'll know where to go this afternoon when hell decides to open its doors."

"Wow. That's colorful." Olivia slipped her hand around Destiny's waist. "Time to put some food in your stomach."

"But there's no food in the house."

Livy encouraged Destiny up the stairs. "No, but there are several restaurants in town."

"But I smell!"

"You won't get an argument from me."

"Thanks."

"We'll find a way. Now out to the car with you."

Destiny struggled to reach the front porch. She dropped to the step and pulled deeply of the vanishing morning's air. Memories were returning with a vengeance. The horse trough was a bathtub and the funny chair, a toilet. This house, too, was coming back to her memory. There'd been wondrous times and heartache. When the young Francesca had lost her love to the fighting in North Africa during the second World War, she was gutted. No amount of ancient wisdom could begin to heal her heart. She pleaded with her mother to be sent to an aunt living in America, but Annemarie would not hear of it.

The great grandmother tightened the house rules and restricted Francesca's movements. In so doing, the inevitable occurred. Destiny was sent to keep the young woman from doing something completely rash.

Young Daniel Kilkenny was an honest, sweet man who wasn't looking to leave his mark on Europe. He was in Sardinia to do his duty to his country and return home in one piece—alive.

Destiny chuckled. Everyone knew when she stepped into the picture, all bets were off. The two young people met, fell in love, and as soon as Danny was able, he paid for Francesca to sail to New York. She willingly left knowing she would never see the island of Sardinia or her family again.

How ironic her granddaughter would return the family back to the island.

She realized she'd woven a tapestry for another pair of lovers but had to put it aside. The woman in the tapestry was born two centuries later than originally planned. Someone in the planning department had fallen asleep on that assignment. She thought she'd never hear the end it.

This time turbulence could put right what a clerical error had created.

# Chapter Nine

Olivia locked the front door and spotted Destiny on the steps. "Why aren't you in the car?"

"I smell?"

"Oh, right. Come on." She helped her new resident up and guided her to the passenger side of the vehicle. Opening the door, she grabbed Destiny's rucksack. "I think it would be best to keep this in the trun…boot, for now. The smell won't be quite so overwhelming."

Destiny nodded and let go of the bag. She quickly surveyed the inside of this automobile. Changes made during the time she'd been elsewhere left her confused; almost as confused as she was the first time she'd seen a gas powered vehicle.

Olivia entered the driver's side and buckled her seat belt. "You too. This car doesn't move until everyone is belted in."

Destiny blanched. A belt for a seat? "I'm sorry. Back home I drive an old car that doesn't have—seat belts. Please show me?"

Livy leaned over Destiny and pulled the metal clasp attached to a— rifle strap—from the retainer across her body, snapping it closed in the silver buckle on her left. "Now we go." She put the auto into gear, and the vehicle lurched forward. When she looked past Destiny to see if the road was clear to enter, she noted the young woman's face was devoid of all color. "You okay?"

"Uhm huh." A weak nod accompanied the answer.

"I called my, cousin, at city hall and asked for a recommendation of where to eat that might allow us to sit outside. She gave me the name of a couple pizzerias. Oh, and she told me where we can go to wash clothes. She's going to have the water turned on at the house, so we can do a more thorough cleaning." Livy looked at her passenger. "And be able to bathe."

Destiny's hands were grasped tightly on the seat edge. Absolute fear emitted from her body in waves.

"Are you scared?" Olivia's brow corrugated in concern.

Destiny cleared her throat. "These roads are so narrow. It gives me pause... and yes, scares me a bit."

"I'm driving the best I know how. Would you like to drive?"

"No, good heavens, no. I can honestly say I've not driven any of the new automobiles and don't wish to start now."

"I guess it's a good thing we're here then, right?" Livy parked the car in front of a building displaying a pizzeria sign.

Destiny hesitated.

"We'll go inside, decide what we want to eat, then go to the patio out back." Livy smiled. "Fair dinkum?"

"Fair dinkum."

The pair took a moment, once they were inside, to adjust to the darkened atmosphere. Destiny was slowly regaining her memory of the language but opted to allow Olivia to take the lead. *No sense in tipping my hand just yet.*

A medium sized, deep dish pizza pie was ordered with the local goat cheese for topping. They walked through the *ristorante* and out the back door, where the order would be delivered to them on the patio. A few folks sat at tables eating and conversing, but neither woman paid attention to them. Rumbling stomachs were demanding food.

Olivia felt the hair on the back of her neck prickle. *Someone is watching us.* She grabbed her mirrored sunglasses and slipped them on.

Destiny watched this action with interest. "I didn't think it was that bright in here."

"It's not. I just have the distinct feeling someone is watching us. Wearing these give me the advantage of being able to see without being seen."

Destiny shook her head. "I know we've just met, but…have you lost your mind?"

Olivia huffed. "Maybe, but I'd rather be safe with a plan of action than not."

Destiny took another bite of the warm pizza. It beat the heck out of hard tack or moldy bread. This assignment might not be so bad, after all.

~ * ~

"Oh, come on, Rafaele. She's a real beauty. Must be a tourist, cause I've never seen her in town before."

Rafaele Sonna grabbed the pepper flakes and liberally added them to his lunch. He concentrated on the food in front of him. His friend and co-worker, Paolo Manca was a notorious lady-killer always on the lookout for a new conquest. However, this girl he'd set his sights on must be something for Paolo to call her a beauty not a babe.

He raised his eyes above his food to sneak a peek. She was leaning over the table to grab something near her plate. She looked up right before donning a pair of mirrored glasses.

He stopped, mesmerized by the hazel eyes. Her clean hair bounced with energy. Something about her manner set her apart from the summer travelers who wandered through town on their various pilgrimages.

"Hot, right?"

Paolo's garlic breath blew across Rafaele's nose. He dropped his eyes to his dish again. There was so much to do to get ready for the Autumn festival. "Paolo, we don't have time for you to try putting another notch on your bedpost."

The man let loose a belch that shook the rafters. "Good pizza. Why not? If, as I suspect, she is a tourist, she'll be gone by the end of the week."

"You assume too much. If she's not a tourist, then what?"

Paolo shrugged his shoulders. "*E la vita*?"

The two men continued in this vein until they'd finished their lunch. They cleaned their table and left.

~ * ~

Destiny watched the soap opera unfold before her eyes. All the players in this drama had been introduced. It was now up to her to start the opening act.

"You've been rather quiet. Sorry if I snipped at you. Guess I was hungrier than I thought."

The dream weaver allowed silence to descend on the table. "Were you snippy? I didn't notice. I was too busy tucking in to this amazing food. Next a bath and getting my clothes clean."

Olivia eyed her with suspicion. "Uhm, right. I agree with you about the bath. I want to check back at the city hall to see if my," she used her fingers to make quote marks, "cousin can help me find a construction company. I hope they'll be able to get the house in living condition before winter hits. I've heard it snows sometimes."

Olivia and Destiny cleaned their table and left the pizzeria.

"The office is just down the street. Let's walk." Setting a brisk pace, Destiny found she was scurrying to keep up.

"What's your hurry?"

"Time is of the essence here."

"Amen."

"What?"

"Nothing."

Angelica expressed surprise at seeing Olivia so soon. "Maybe I should hire you to work here?"

The pair exchanged smiles. Olivia pulled out her phone. "Angelica, would you be able to direct me to a local contractor who is honest, reliable, and fairly priced? I know that is a lot to ask, but I have no idea where to start looking?"

Angelica pulled her round card file toward her and quickly rifled through the small cards. *"Ecco.* These guys are local. They work on all our town festival buildings and live in the district. Oh, when you contact

Rafaele, have him call me."

"Thank you." Livy entered the information into her cell phone. She and Destiny turned to leave.

"Oh, yes. I wanted to let you know I contacted the American Embassy to file a missing report on your friend. Also, the water company will be out in a couple days to hook up your pipes. The electric..." she shrugged her shoulders and held her hands palms up. "It might take a bit longer."

Olivia thanked her and herded Destiny outside.

Having done what she could for the time being, Livy decided she and Destiny would return to the hotel where she was temporarily staying. A shower and washing her clothes would be a priority for the traveler. "Let's go to my hotel. You can freshen up and wash your clothes while we set a plan in place."

"Sounds heavenly."

The pair climbed into Olivia's rental vehicle and made the brief journey to the hotel.

When Destiny had showered and cleaned her "modern" clothing, she tossed the 19th century garb into a rubbish bag then carried it out to the community can.

They took bottles of water out and sat beneath the oaks in the yard.

"I'd like to ask, if I may, to refurbish the loom in the cellar. Weaving relaxes me after a day of digging in the dirt and tromping around the landscape." Destiny waited anxiously for Olivia's reply.

"Sure. It looks to be in fairly good condition. Letting it rot would be such a waste."

Destiny breathed a relieved sigh. "Thank you."

"Do you have anything specific in mind to weave?"

A smile snuck across Destiny's lips. "I do, but it's a gift so, don't ask any more questions. You'll spoil the surprise."

"I love presents!" Olivia's eyes sparkled.

*If you only knew...*

# Chapter Ten

Olivia's finger hesitated over the number. *What if he thinks I've lost my mind?*

"You can what if yourself to death but that won't get the house in shape." Destiny slung her rucksack over her shoulder.

"Where are you going?" Livy's forehead furrowed.

"It's just a jaunt down the road and unless you've locked the house, I'll be going to work on the loom."

"I did lock the house. Let me drive you. I can call from there just as well as here." She grabbed her purse and the ever-present notebook, moving to the door.

"You don't really have to go if you don't want to. Just let me have the key, and I'll make sure to lock up when I leave to go to the ruins."

"No. I don't know what I would do here. Sitting and drinking all day is not my idea of a good time. Besides, this is my home now. I need to start considering it as such. The sooner I dive into making repairs and establishing myself in the community, the sooner I'll be accepted as an Ollollain."

Destiny agreed. "You have a point."

The pair walked to the car and were at the house before they could engage the air conditioner. Creeping up the driveway, Destiny noted Olivia stiffening at the sight of a pickup truck parked in front of the home. The ladder racks and toolbox implicated builders of some sort, a logo with R & P Construzioni on the door.

"Who the…?"

Clambering out of the vehicle, Olivia strode to the steps to question the two men seated and drinking coffee. "Who are you and what are you doing at my home?"

Paolo looked to Rafaele. *"Che cosa ha detto?"*

Rafaele held up a hand. "My name is Rafaele Sonna and this is Paolo. I'm sorry for not contacting you first, *signorina*. Signora Porcu at the mayor's office called me yesterday and told me you might be in need of a builder. She was wrong?"

Olivia shook her head. "No. I do need a builder, but I thought… Wait a minute. You speak English."

Rafaele smiled. "Some. It did not escape my attention, as a young man, just how many visitors to our small island spoke the unfamiliar tongue. I knew if I was to be successful, I would need to learn this language."

Destiny stood a couple steps behind Olivia watching the scene unfold. *This is going better than I'd hoped.*

"I do need a builder to bring the house to a livable state, but I'm not looking to change the basic format."

Rafaele turned and translated to Paolo what had been said.

"Oh, great. An American who wants to *live like the locals*. She'll probably be looking for a husband and bambinos too. She's all yours." Paolo rolled his eyes and drew circles in the dirt on the porch.

"For your *informazioni, signore*, I have no need for a husband." Olivia watched the swarthy man's cheeks drain of color. "Yes, I know some Sardinian. My nonna taught me enough to understand more than I can speak. If I decide to use your services, please keep your comments to yourself."

Livy stomped up the steps and unlocked the door. She swung it open and powered through to the kitchen area. Destiny hung back to overhear the conversation between the two men.

"You are such an idiot, Paolo. If we lose this job because of your mouth…" Rafaele shook his head, following Olivia into the house.

Paolo tagged along behind his enthusiasm visibly lacking. He muttered beneath his breath and huffed his way into the house. *If I didn't need this job…*

Destiny caught up to Olivia. "I'm going to head to the cellar and assess the loom. I brought your torch and will be able to see with it. If you need me," she turned and looked at the young men, "for anything, just call." She set off for the basement. As the sun rose in the sky, the temperature followed suit. While the upper house was currently at a comfortable temperature, it would soon begin to drift upward to stuffy and hot. Being in the cellar suited the weaver just fine.

Olivia watched Rafaele walk the kitchen, testing light switches, faucets and windows. He wrote in a notebook similar to hers.

"This house is in remarkably good condition. I think you will only need to update the plumbing and electrical to make it livable. I would recommend replacing these old windows and considering new doors."

"And how much is this basic work going to cost me?" Olivia allowed skepticism to creep into her answer.

Rafaele wrote a figure on his notebook and showed it to her.

"Are you serious?"

"*Si.* Is there a problem?"

"No, I just, well, it's very economical."

"*Si.* Why would it be otherwise?"

"Because I'm American?"

"How does that help me? I live in this community too. We would see each other at the festivals and shopping. If I were to disrespect you, your cousin would have my head on a stick."

"Ah, Angelica."

"Yes. She is but one of the *many* Porcus in this city and region."

"Including me."

"That is what she tells me."

"Well, I guess she's right."

Rafaele looked at Olivia. He was having a difficult time trying to understand what it was she wanted. Of course, these were the rates he charged all his customers. He bit back any negative remarks. "If you wish to consider other builders, I'll be happy to provide names for you."

Livy shook her head. "No, no. That's not what I meant. Listen," she pushed an exasperated sigh through her lips. *Sometimes I'm such an idiot.* "Would you walk through the other rooms with me to determine if there are any other major changes needing attention?"

"Of course." He waved his hand for her to lead the way.

Paolo looked over the room, opening a cabinet door or two, then hurrying to catch up with Rafaele and the American woman. This would be money in the bank for very little work. Just what he liked.

Destiny closed the basement door, feeling the handset catch. "Lock." She flicked on the torch and followed the beam of light to the corner. She had ripped up her 19$^{th}$ century shirt to use as a dusting rag. "Wind." Blowing through her lips cleared the majority of cobwebs, but there was still work to be done to get the loom ready for use. Destiny found a wooden crate. She set the flashlight on it facing toward the loom. "Bright." More illumination brightened the corner occupied by the large tool.

She took her rag, the one imbued with her scent, and wiped all the wooden pieces of the loom. With each swipe, the warmth of the creation sprung to life. Destiny grabbed the torch from the wooden box and slid the box to the machine. She climbed up, hoping against hope it wouldn't break, and continued to gently, lovingly clean the rug creator. "Pray tell, my beauty, what is your name?"

"*Sogno tessitore.*"

"Dream weaver. We have a connection. I would ask you to help me unite two people who need each other. One is returning home, the other needs his own home. You and I can make this happen. Will you help?"

"*Sì.*"

"Thank you." She stepped back and gazed at the loom before her. The mastery of work applied to it required her to do her best work. "And that I will."

The sound of rattling broke her reverie, and she realized someone was trying to come into the cellar. "Open."

"Destiny?"

"Yes?"

"Are you alright? I couldn't get the door to open."

"I'm fine. Door's probably just a bit swollen from the early morning damp."

Olivia and Rafaele entered the basement and moved to Destiny. "Wow. My flashlight really puts out a lot of light, doesn't it?"

Destiny silently cursed. "Yes. Must be lithium batteries."

"Could be." Olivia faced Rafaele. "See? Isn't this amazing? I don't understand how this thing could survive all these years of neglect." She moved to the loom and touched the recently cleaned wood. "Oh, my. It absolutely glows." Her hand stroked the uprights and she stepped back to look at the complete machine. "I almost wish I knew how to weave."

Rafaele stood watching the American marvel at something he'd always taken for granted. "You don't have a loom in your home?"

Olivia shook her head negatively. "America is the land of throw-away. Most of those who weave, at least where I'm from, do it for art. Not for clothing." She stepped back. "I think it's time to set this plan into motion. Destiny?"

Olivia ambled to the steps. Rafaele following with Destiny close at his heels. When the trio exited the cellar, Rafaele looked around in an attempt to locate his co-worker. "Paolo?"

The man entered the front door, exhaling a stream of smoke. *"Si?"*

Olivia froze in horror. "Please. No smoking in the house; *per favore, non fumare en casa."*

Rafaele watched a shadow of annoyance pass over his friend's face.

*"Mi dispiace.* I'm sorry." Paolo tromped out the door and flicked his cigarette off the porch.

Rafaele smacked his forehead with the palm of his hand. *"Idiota."* He marched out the front door, found the butt, and ground out the lit end before picking it up and putting it in his pocket. He walked back to the house, commenting as he passed Paolo, "We'll talk about this."

Paolo huffed. "Yeah, whatever." He strode to the truck where he lit another cigarette and blew smoke upward. "Americans."

"Please excuse my co-worker. While we work on your home, there will be no smoking in the house. Will that be acceptable?"

Olivia nodded a yes. "I'd appreciate if you didn't smoke around the porch either. Please."

"Of course, *signorina*. I need to go to my office and complete an estimate for the work to be done on your home. May I call you when it's complete?"

"Sure." She opened the notebook and pulled a business card from the left side pocket. Scribbling on the back of the card, she added her cell number. "This is my phone. Please call me as soon as you have the numbers. I'll need time to consider the costs and make my decision."

*"Si, signorina."* Rafaele took the card and placed it into his top shirt pocket. He walked to his pickup truck where Paolo stood puffing away on another cigarette. "You know, you really are an idiot? Are you trying to lose us this job? I was under the impression you needed the money."

Paolo glared at Rafaele as he pulled in deeply of the cigarette. "What makes you think I need this job?"

"I've had to pay off your tab at the pizzeria—again. This is getting old, Paolo."

He shrugged his shoulders. "I didn't have a papa who sent me away to school. I couldn't afford a college education. You've got the money, and I'll pay you back."

"Not likely. You had the grades and the brains to go to school. I know they waive fees for those who don't have the funding in some cases. You just didn't want to leave Ollolai because of Genisse."

"So?"

"What did it get you? She married D'Agostino anyway. Let's go. I have work to do."

As the pair opened the doors to the pickup, they heard their names being called. Rafaele watched Olivia sprinting to the truck. When she arrived, she stopped, leaned over and placed her hands on her knees as she tried to catch her breath.

"Please…wait a minute." When she'd recovered, she stood and leaned against the truck fender.

"I wouldn't…" Rafaele started but failed to stop her action. "It's really dirty."

Olivia smiled. "No biggie."

The odd expression received raised eyebrows from the pair.

"What did you need, *signorina*?" Paolo attempted a neutral tone to his voice.

"I wonder if I might ask you to do me a favor?" Her hazel eyes hooded with worry.

"We will try. What would that be?" Rafaele lay an arm across the open door of the truck.

"Well, my friend Taylor is missing."

"Your friend is a tailor?" Paolo was puzzled.

"No." Olivia could see the language barrier causing a problem. "My friend's name is Taylor. Here's her picture." She opened her wallet to a picture receiving a great deal of attention lately. It was Olivia and Taylor leaning against the railing along the Willamette River in Portland during Fleet Week. The sun was highlighting the pair, and they were giggling about some private joke. It was before the news Taylor's fiancé was MIA. "She came along on this trip with me but…"

The men could see something was bothering the American *signorina*. She straightened and started speaking again.

"About a week ago, we arrived and settled at the hotel. I knew I wanted to see the house as soon as possible, but she wasn't as excited. After all, this is *my* home. She was only considering staying. Not important now. She decided to take the day and go sailing. She took her rental car and left. I've not seen her since that day. The local police have been notified, and my—cousin—made out a report for the American Embassy. She's just, disappeared. If you are on the east side of the island, will you please keep your eyes open for her? If she's hurt and can't remember her name or something, I'll drop everything I'm doing to come get her."

Rafaele pursed his lips. "You say she told you she was going—

sailing?"

Livy nodded. "She wanted to see the Spanish watch posts."

"Last week in the afternoon." He turned and gave Paolo a knowing look. The pair responded in tandem. "Mediterranean Mist."

"What?"

"In the summer, our beautiful ocean hides a secret known only to those living in the area. The sky is blue, and clouds appear white and fluffy. Around two or three o'clock, a storm blows in and steals unwary sailors from their vessels. They disappear and are never seen again. We call it the Mediterranean Mist."

"Oh, please." Olivia scoffed at such an idea. *Mediterranean Mist.*

"Does not your country have the Bermuda Triangle?" Paolo tilted his head slightly.

"Yes, but..."

"Is it not the same there? People go in and don't come back?" He lifted a brow.

"Uh, I, guess."

"I'm afraid your friend has become one more person to disappear in the Mist."

"We'll look for your friend, as requested," Rafaele answered. "But I think she has arrived at her destination already; wherever that may be." The men crawled into the truck and drove away.

Olivia returned to the house, mindlessly roaming through the rooms. She pulled the old broom from the closet in the kitchen and went to the furthest room. She started her campaign there. Every cobweb, dust mote and foreign object was cleansed from the area and escorted to the outside by the broom. As her mind tumbled through the ideas implanted by the men, Livy experienced a deep, unfamiliar ache in her chest.

A hand gently touched her shoulder. "Are you alright?" Destiny seemed to sense the turmoil roiling through Olivia's mind.

"I guess." She walked to the front porch and sat on the top step. "Taylor is the closest thing I have to a best friend. I'd really hoped she would decide to stay on in Sardinia. I don't know too many soldiers who return from the battlefields, alive, after being listed as missing in action."

Destiny took a seat next to Livy. "It does happen occasionally, but not often. Could she have opted to return to the Colonies without her stuff?"

Olivia contemplated the thought. "She might have, but her passport is in the room. I suspect traveling without one isn't easy."

The weaver patted her benefactor on the shoulder. "Why don't you go back to the hotel, get a meal and wait to hear from the contractor? I've a feeling he'll bring some good news. I need to get into the field, again, for my research. I'll be sure to lock the door any time I leave. If you allow me to keep the torch, I'll have some light when it gets dark…if I stay awake that long." Destiny graced Olivia with a smile.

Olivia stood. "I could sure use some good news about now. I think I'll have the staff let me into Taylor's room to gather her items. If she comes back in the next day or two, we can double up in the bed. Otherwise…" she allowed the thought to die. With luck, tomorrow would be the start of reconstruction of the Porcu villa in Ollolai.

# Chapter Eleven

Paolo asked Rafaele to drop him in the center of town. "I'll walk home."

"You sure?"

*"Si.* Call me when it's time to work."

"Okay."

Paolo watched the truck rumble down the street and disappear around a corner before he pulled out his phone. He punched in the number and waited.

*"Pronto?"*

"Genisse?"

*"Si."*

"I need two drops, as soon as you can. I've business in Nuoro."

"Problem?"

"Not if you make the drops in the next thirty minutes. Otherwise, yes."

*"Capisco. Caio."*

*"Caio."*

Paolo jogged the five blocks to his house. He quickly threw together clothing for a weekend away. Locking his home, he used the stairs from the kitchen to the garage. Opening the door, he stepped out and scanned the road. Determining there were no other vehicles utilizing the street, Paolo backed out his Fiat 124 Spider. He turned from the driver seat and used the remote to close the garage. Once secured, he put the vehicle in gear and maneuvered the back streets to No. 129 straight into Nuovo. If Rafaele called him for work, oh well.

~ * ~

Olivia spoke with the front desk and notified them of her plans regarding Tay's things. It was the height of tourist season. She surmised they would have no trouble filling the vacancy. Her task filled but half an hour as she checked the room and adjoining bathroom twice hoping against hope Tay would walk in and get pissed at her "rummaging" through her things.

Olivia meandered to the *ristorante* and ordered the lunch special with a local wine. She opted to sit outside and consider the current situation. It really wasn't like Tay to walk away without explanation. That was why Olivia was so worried. Tay said she'd be back. But her things now resided in Livy's room. As completely ridiculous as the local legend seemed, it was the only explanation making any sense at all.

~ * ~

Rafaele ran the numbers twice. He was ready to give Signorina Martin an estimate. He called her cell and received the voice mail. "Hate this thing," he muttered. "Signorina, please contact me when you get my message. I have an estimate I believe will work for both of us. Caio." There was nothing else he could do but wait.

~ * ~

Olivia took a sip of wine and glanced at her phone. "Damn. I have a message. Maybe from Tay?" Her heart started pounding as she hoped. The message was from Rafaele with a quote on the remodel. "That has to be wrong. Maybe it's without building a garage. I'll need to talk to him for clarification." She dialed the number he left. He answered after the first ring.

*"Pronto?"*

"Rafaele? It's Olivia. I have a few questions regarding this quote."

*"Si.* How can I help?"

"I don't wish to sound ungrateful, but these prices are so reasonable I'm wondering if they include the garage I wanted to have built?" Olivia heard the groan at the other end of the phone.

"No, *dispiace.* A garage would be an additional $5000 Euros."

"Hmm. How about a three-sided carport?"

*"Que cosa?* Sorry, what?"

Olivia sighed. "I think we really need to get together. I'll explain what a carport is when you bring a contract for me to sign; at the house around ten in the morning?"

"I will have the paperwork ready. We can talk about this…carport at that time. *Ciao."*

*"Ciao."*

Olivia breathed relief. She had a contractor for the refurbishing and a—cousin—willing to ride roughshod over him if he considered committing fraud or presenting inferior work. She couldn't help but wonder why her grandmother had been in such a hurry to leave this place. *No matter. I'm back and planting my roots in this Sardinian soil.*

~ * ~

Rafaele pushed back in his chair. He needed to call Salvatore's Supply and see about setting up an order. The supply line to Sardinia was sometimes…more relaxed than he would like. He picked up the phone and dialed the familiar number.

"Salvatore? It's Rafaele. *Bion giorno."*

*"Bion giorno."*

Rafaele was taken back. Salvatore was normally jovial and chatty. Today, he seemed—reticent.

"I would like to order some supplies for a job I have coming up. Can I do that through you?"

"I'm sorry, Rafaele. I can't preorder supplies any longer."

"May I ask why?"

"I've had issues with some of my accounts not paying in a timely manner…"

"But I always make sure Genisse pays you first."

"I know. However, I can't make an exception. As small as this town is, well, you understand. Yes?"

Rafaele didn't understand completely, but it was Salvatore's business, and unless he wanted to go all the way to Nuoro to buy supplies, he'd abide by the man's decision.

*"Si.* May I write you a check? I know there is plenty in the company account. You can contact the bank before they close today. Will that work?" He felt the hesitation on the other man's part.

"Okay. I'll take the check and call the bank. If it is verified…"

"When…"

"When it has been verified, we can go from there."

"Fine. I'll be at the shop soon. *Ciao.*"

*"Ciao."*

Rafaele experienced the hair on the back of his neck bristle. "What is going on?" He grabbed his checkbook and headed to Salvatore's. Maybe the man would be more forthcoming in a face to face encounter. He'd calculated the cost of the initial work would run around $2000 EU. He was owed money from a couple other jobs completed in the last month, so liquidity was not an issue.

Pulling in front of the store, Rafaele parked his truck and ambled inside. He headed for the electrical department to check if the modern switches would work with what he suspected was ancient wiring. *Won't know until I open an electrical box.* He was examining several other wiring necessities when Salvatore approached him.

"Rafaele."

"Salvatore."

"How much do you want to write your check for?"

"I'd like to make it for $2000 EU and have what I don't use

immediately put on my account. Is that doable for you?"

The storeowner nodded affirmatively. "I do want to check with the bank."

Rafaele agreed. The man's insistence at making sure his check was covered was becoming irritating. They'd been doing business for the last ten years. What had suddenly changed? He wrote the check. "Here you go." As Salvatore trundled to the back office, Rafaele wandered to the plumbing section of the store. He was examining new designs for the toilets when Salvatore appeared at his side, check in hand.

"I'm sorry, Rafaele, but the bank says this is not covered." He watched disbelief cover his client's face.

"But, how?"

"I don't know. The lady at the bank just said there was not enough to cover the check."

Rafaele stiffened. "Will you be open for the next hour?"

"Yes."

"I'll be back with cash. Will that work for you?"

Salvatore nodded.

"Good. Oh yes. Don't work with anyone but me until I tell you otherwise. No Paolo, no Genisse; just me."

"Understood."

"Thank you."

Rafaele walked to the bank and drew from his personal funds. He brought the money to Salvatore. "Remember, I will be the only contact you work with from R & P Construction."

Salvatore sighed as he shook his head. "Yes, just you."

The short ride to the offices of R & P Construction only exacerbated Rafaele's anger. *How could this happen?* Exiting his vehicle, he slammed the door and stomped through the entry. Genisse looked up from her magazine. "Everything all right, boss?"

"No, it's…" Rafaele halted. *Calm. Until you have all the facts, stay calm.* "Just a trying morning. That's all."

"Okay." She didn't sound convinced but seemed hesitant to inquire further. "Paolo called to say he has some personal business that will keep him away from Ollolai until Monday."

"Fine." *Whose wife is garnering his attention, now?* "If he calls back, let him know I'll contact him when there is work to be done."

Genisse set the magazine on the desk. "Of course. Do you wish me to stay?"

Rafaele turned abruptly, several words crowding his thoughts, and slowly breathed out. "No, thank you. I have a few minor tasks to complete, but there really is no need for you to be here. I can grab the phone myself. Have a good weekend, Genisse."

"You, too, boss." She gathered her purse and left the office. "I believe something is going to explode, and it won't be Vesuvius this time."

# Chapter Twelve

Paolo babied the sports car through the back streets of Ollolai, easing it into the garage. Tonight, the door slid quietly on the track to the closed position. So far, everything was going smoothly, except for the panicked call he'd received from Genisse.

"Paolo, he knows! I swear. I just stepped out for a cigarette…"

"I thought you quit."

"Well, I didn't. D'Agostino has no issue with it."

"Whatever."

"Anyway, by the time he'd come in the back door and left again, I was just finishing my smoke. I didn't really see him but when he returned, he was fuming."

"Did he say anything?"

"No, but he was clenching his teeth."

"Look, if he didn't question you, I wouldn't worry. It's when he starts asking questions that we need to panic." Paolo convinced her things would work out to their advantage. It was after this panicked call he made the decision to slow his plan down. By Monday, the situation would be no different than it was the prior week.

He was getting ready to crawl into bed when his cell phone rang. He checked the readout. *Good Lord, now what?* "Hello, Genisse. What do you need?"

"Rafaele told me to pass along this message. Don't come into work. He'll contact you when there is a job to do. Goodnight, Paolo."

Before he could respond, she'd hung up. This wasn't like Rafaele.

Paolo realized now was probably a good time to start worrying.

~ * ~

Destiny fit the final piece into the loom. Standing back to admire the beauty of the pieces, she pulled the fine yarn from her bag to begin the process of setting up the machine for weaving. The threads held no color and shimmered in the light of the flashlight. Having done this for several lifetimes, Destiny was aware the color would tint the tapestry as the assignment, and weaving, neared the finish. "I'm going to need more thread."

A whisper answered. "You'll have all you need. Just ask when you are close to running out."

"I'm taking a leave of absence after this assignment."

"Mmm. Not so fast."

"What?"

"There is another—client—right there on the island. Since you are so near..."

"You're joking, right?"

"We don't joke."

"Fine. Then I want half a century vacation at a location of my choice."

There was a long silence. Destiny began to think she might have pushed her luck.

"Fine. Until..."

"I also want the finest wool, spun and ready to weave, without any red tape attached."

Again, the long silence.

"Alright. We'll be in touch."

She grumbled lowly. Anything louder would have brought unwanted attention her way. *Not what I need.* She checked her bag and, just as promised, new, finely spun threads waited for her to apply to the loom. She closed her bag and grabbed the light. A tickling sensation at the back of her neck alerted her to the fact Olivia might appear. *Best not tempt her.* Opening the door, she saw lights flash across the room. If it wasn't Olivia, they'd be very sorry. She might not have powerful magic, but what she did possess, she knew how to manipulate to her advantage.

A timid voice called out. "Destiny? It's Olivia. I brought dinner. I thought you might be hungry."

"On my way."

They met in the living room and opted to eat out on the porch to enjoy the evening's temperate atmosphere.

"You know, I'm going to have to buy a dining table and chairs. Until my furniture arrives from the states, there really is nothing to sit on or use for eating. I can't imagine trying to write your thesis on the floor."

Destiny grinned. "No, but we archeology-types tend to make-do with what we have. You never know where we'll wind up digging. Hmm. Something smells heavenly."

Olivia giggled. "You can't beat the Italians at their own game. Pasta from heaven; fettuccini. I think I'm in love."

As the pair dug into their meal, conversation lulled. Once they sated their hunger, Olivia began.

"I wanted to let you know what's going to happen. I have a meeting with Rafaele tomorrow around tenish to sign a contract and get the work started. We might walk the house one more time, so we can agree on a working schedule."

Destiny wanted to jump up and down. This assignment was finally moving forward. "Do you need me to do anything? I've a site I want to explore down the road. I'll need to get an early start to avoid the heat of the day."

"Do you want me to drive you there?" Olivia picked up the paper plates and plastic silverware. She put them back into the bag to dispose of when she returned to the hotel.

"No, thanks. After this scrumptious meal, I really think I will need to walk it off."

Olivia chuckled. "Too true. Well, it has been a very long day, and

I'm bushed. Do you need anything before I take off?"

"No. I guess I'll see you sometime tomorrow?"

"Yes. Sleep well, Destiny."

"You, too, Olivia."

The pair parted ways; Destiny returning to the inside of the house as a watch person and Olivia heading back to the hotel less than a mile away.

Destiny slid down a wall and blew out a sigh. She really was in need of a vacation.

# Chapter Thirteen

Rafaele rose with the sun. Years of working construction had ingrained the early to bed, early to rise ritual. He made coffee and breakfast. The newspaper was full of the usual political government misdeeds. *So glad I opted not to live on the mainland.* Once he cleaned up his dishes, he went to his home office and printed out the contracts he would need to have Olivia sign. His plan was to check with the bank first thing this morning. He wanted a copy of all the business transactions for the last year. If the account had errors, he wanted to see if it was a one off or if this was a pattern. If it was the latter of the two, he wanted to track it and find out why.

He was the first in the lobby and first at the teller window. "Morning, Cecelia." As with many of the businesspeople in Ollolai, Rafaele and Cecelia had attended school at the same time.

"Morning, Rafaele. How can I help you this morning?"

"I'd like to check the balance of the company account, please."

"Give me a minute to look it up." She ran the name through the computer and brought up R & P Construction. "Here you go. Would you like me to write down the balance?"

Rafaele nodded.

"Okay." She took a notepad and put the number showing on the bottom line. She slid the paper across the counter to him.

Heat flooded his face. "Are you sure?"

Cecelia motioned him to come closer to the counter. She turned the computer toward him so he could see the screen. "As you can see, the number here is the one I put on the paper for you."

Rafaele straightened up. "Would you please print me out all the transactions for this account during the past year?"

She waved toward a seating arrangement facing the town square. "Of course, Rafaele. It might take about ten minutes or so to get the year's business. I'll bring it to you in the sitting area. Will that be sufficient?"

He realized he must have looked quite dour because she was speaking rather formally. Rafaele smiled. "Yes, that will be perfect. Thank you so much for your trouble."

She returned his smile. "Not a problem."

He took a seat and watched as the small-town center began to come to life. The numbers she'd written and shown him were more than sufficient to cover the amount of supplies he'd wanted to purchase from Salvatore's. The bank, and for that matter, Salvatore, didn't make mistakes as obvious as the one from Friday. The whole situation irritated him to no end. Keeping the accounts up to date and current was part of Genisse's job. Was it time for an office overhaul?

He sure hoped not. Cecelia brought out a manila file folder containing a healthy amount of paperwork.

"If you need anything else, call me." She handed him a card with her number and extension listed. "Have a good day, Raffy."

He grinned at her. The nickname from school hadn't been used in many years. Signing the contracts with Olivia was his next step. He placed the bank paperwork in his briefcase then left the bank. Much as he hated paperwork, it appeared he was going to be forced to perform a complete audit of his business—alone.

~ * ~

Olivia moved the stone next to the esparto plant to find the key right where Destiny stated she would leave it. As the door squeaked open, she sensed a calmness about the house she'd not noticed prior. Destiny must have opened windows to allow the fresh air to permeate the rooms.

Whatever it was gave her a sense of welcome.

The few people in the Northwest she considered friends had been aghast that she would leave a successful career and move to "a foreign country." They didn't really understand. She was the daughter of a daughter of an immigrant. When her mother was at her wit's end with Olivia, she would never fail to remind her of said fact.

"Do not get uppity with me, young lady. I'll ship you back to Nonna's homeland in the blink of an eye. We'll see how you like it there!"

Well, here she was wishing her mother had made good on the threat. What she had witnessed so far was more of the lifestyle she would have preferred. Puttering around the kitchen area, Olivia heard a vehicle crunching up the drive. She peeked out the front window to witness Rafaele's pickup parking. She had brought some cleaning items with her to get started on removing the first decade or so of dirt. Using a rag, she cleared a spot on the hutch. "That should work."

Rafaele parked his truck. He grabbed the briefcase and walked to the porch of the home. Before he could lift a hand to knock on the door, it opened. Olivia smiled and invited him inside. She directed him to the kitchen area and indicated he should place his items on the sideboard.

He opened his case and retrieved a sheaf of papers from the interior. Olivia's eyes widened. "Wow."

He held up a hand. "Please don't panic. I have two sets of paperwork; one for you and one for me. I've also made sure to print the contract in Italian AND English. All legal papers here are in Italian. I don't wish to have any misunderstandings between us."

"Thank you. I appreciate your honesty."

The pair spent the next forty-five minutes going over the specifics of exactly what was to be repaired, projected time schedules, and the days and times work would commence. During this review, Rafaele did his best to explain the idiosyncrasies of Italian laws and how they would affect the work. "If you wish we can go to the bank and I'll resign while Cecelia witnesses and verifies the signature. She is a *notaio pubblico. Capice?"*

"Public notary?"

*"Si.* She is that."

A grin tugged at the corners of Olivia's mouth. "I believe we can both agree to honor the contract as stated. After all, we live in the same town and will see each other at town events and while shopping."

"This is a truth. Now…I'd like to inspect the electrical outlets again. Would that be acceptable?"

"Of course. I'm wanting to go over some of the house and rethink the possibilities. Maybe, with a bit more funding, I can have some modifications made. Maybe…"

Olivia made her way to the second floor. She'd been thinking about the house layout and wanted to keep the bedroom facing the town for herself. If she could convince the contractor to put in a small balcony, it would serve as a perfect place to enjoy a glass of wine in the evening and watch the sunset. The current windows were swollen in place, and she was afraid if she forced them open the old timber frames would split. It seemed simple enough to just cut to the floor level and put in French doors. Considering the improvements in the design and installation of the modern windows, she should be able to have the view and the heat in wintertime, too.

She slowly descended the stairs, consciously testing the railings. They were solid. *One less item to worry about.* On the ground floor, a trip to the kitchen informed her Rafaele was still inside. His briefcase was open, papers scattered. She fought the urge to inspect the documents. Out of curiosity, she stepped to the sink and turned on the faucet. The ensuing screeching brought Rafaele from his location at a run.

"What the…?"

Livy blushed. "I just wanted to see if the water had been turned on. It would make cleaning a great deal easier." The pipes shuttered and hissed, red dust pouring into the basin. After several minutes of excruciating noises, the liquid flowing began to clear in color. The cloud of dust settled, and dust became mud, which became water. Still retaining a hint of red, the liquid sputtered as pipes not utilized in seventy years were, once again, employed. Olivia allowed the pipe to stay open until the water ran clear.

Once there were no longer particulates in the stream, she cupped her hand and sipped. "That is heavenly. I can't remember tasting water so—sweet."

Rafaele nodded. "We are very fortunate to have the best water in the region. The rocks over which the streams pass act as filters, taking out the bad taste and giving us this bit of heaven."

Olivia held her hands beneath the faucet, rubbing her thumbs over her fingertips. "This is so pristine. My hands feel soft." She turned off the kitchen water. "I need to check the bathrooms."

She darted off. Rafaele could hear the same screeching noises then a prolonged period of water running. The next half hour followed in the same manner. When he saw Olivia next, she was smiling. "Everything okay?"

"Yes. I'm one step closer to moving into my home. Oh, Rafaele, I'd like to ask you about a small change I'd like to have made upstairs. Do you have time?"

"Of course, *signorina.* What are you thinking of doing?"

As she led him upstairs to what was to be the master bedroom, she launched into her idea about the balcony and French doors. "You'll see. It has the most amazing view…"

# Chapter Fourteen

Destiny could hear the conversation from above but wasn't interested enough to snoop. Olivia and Rafaele were probably just putting finishing touches on their contract negotiations.

"Light."

The room brightened, and Destiny took her place at the loom. She picked up the shuttle, running her fingers over the fine wood. "Best get started." Continuing where she'd left off the previous day, she slipped the tool between layers of the finest spun wool fibers the mortal world had seen. Right to left, left to right, repeat. After every two lines of weaving, she would use the beater to batten the threads against material already created.

The routine took on a rhythm. Right to left, left to right, right to left, left to right, batten. She'd been weaving for half an hour when she noticed threads in the material nearest her were breaking. Not completely ripping away from the body of the tapestry but unraveling ever so slowly.

"Oh, goddess. What's happening now?"

About the time she set the shuttle on the beater, she noticed the same threads reweaving into the design. "If this continues, I see I'll need to step in and set these two straight. The sooner they start on the path chosen for them, the sooner I can move on to my other assignment, then…a much needed break."

The end of her sentence was punctuated with the slam of a heavy door followed by skittering of rocks in front of the house. She sighed. "Why couldn't an assignment be easy, just for once?" Back to the loom she trotted to see if she could repair the damage and get ahead of things. It wasn't until her stomach growled, echoing through the cellar, did she decide to stop for the evening. A loaf of bread with a bit of cheese would, should, quiet her system. She recalled hearing the clanging of pipes earlier and surmised the water must be usable and flowing.

Shuttle between the weft, she spoke two words. "Secure," then "Dark." The candles flickered out plunging the cellar into darkness. Destiny skulked about the hallway, peeking around corners and listening for sounds of others. When she stopped to view the living area, the only movement was the dust motes waltzing across sunbeams streaming through the windows.

Paperwork scattered across the hutch caught her attention. Two signed contracts were opened to the material breakdown and cost pages. "He may verbally deny his attraction but the extra steps he's taken to ensure she understands the contracts show his true feelings." The two sets of papers were in Italian, the legal language of Sardinia, and English.

She moved to the sink and turned on the faucet. Waiting for several minutes, she was rewarded with cool, clear water, which she used to wash off the dust collected in the cellar. As the day was quickly warming, Destiny chose to dry off on the front porch. She picked up the key from the handy hiding place. By the time she sat on the step, her arms were dry, and her eyelids were heading toward her cheeks. A nap seemed a very good idea.

~ * ~

Olivia pushed into her room. "That man!" He could be a charming devil one moment and an argumentative ass the next. "I'm not sure I'm going to make it through this remodel without killing him." There were few options, though, so she was going to have to find a way to control her temper and tongue. She flung her body on the bed and stared at the ceiling. "Hmm. Maybe a skylight?" She allowed her mind to play with the idea. She was sure Rafaele would nix it citing building regulations, money and time considerations. And what was all this nonsense about bearing walls? Weren't all the walls bearing the weight of the roof?

Okay, so she wasn't totally construction savvy. He still didn't need to get so…excited. Guess it was just his Sardinian blood, but, wait a minute. She was Sardinian too. His face turned a funny shade of red when she mentioned putting in a Romeo balcony. How frigging difficult could it be to knock out a portion of the wall, hang a balcony and support it? As far as she could see, not very, however, he went on about a bearing wall, and scaffolding to hold up the workers, and time, and money, and on, and on.

She really wanted to go over that contract again. She was having second thoughts about hiring him. Livy traveled back to the car to pick up the paperwork. Once opening the door and facing the empty seat, she realized she'd left the paperwork back at the house. "Damn it."

Walking seemed to be a logical solution. It wouldn't kill her and might just soothe the irritation she was currently feeling. Halfway to the house, the sweat beads rolling down her back had her thinking she'd made a mistake deciding to hike the short distance. The house rose up on the horizon and Livy let out a sigh of relief. At least she'd be able to sit in the shade and cool down before heading back to the hotel. She spied a form on the porch. *Who…?*

Trudging up the driveway, dirt crunching beneath her shoes, the mysterious person took on a familiar look. *Why is Destiny sleeping outside?* Olivia's big city fear meter kicked in. *What if…stop. This is Sardinia. Everybody in town knows, and most likely is related to, the next person.*

She sat on the step and gently touched the young student's shoulder. "Destiny? It's Olivia."

The weaver woke with a start. "What? Where am I?"

Livy gawked at Destiny. "I thought you were English?"

She cleared her throat. "I am. Why?"

"You said something when you opened your eyes, but I have no idea what it was. You were talking in some weird language." Olivia watched the woman flush to her toes.

"Sorry. My parents were from Eastern Europe. We spoke Chechen

66

at home."

"Oh. Why were you sleeping on the porch?"

"I walked in from the main road after spending time at the new, to me, site, and was just intending to sit for a few minutes. You saw what happened." The pink color creeping up her neck matched the embarrassed look on her face.

Livy bit her lip to keep from smiling. "I did, indeed. What say we go inside so I can pick up the contract and go over it with time to check out the fine details? Afterward, pasta?"

Destiny stood and stretched. "Sounds wonderful. Have you connected the stove to a power source?"

Oliva groaned. "No. I guess it's a good thing there are a couple good restaurants in town. We'll head to one of those."

"They are, after all, the experts. Oh, here." She handed the key to Olivia.

The pair entered the house where Olivia retrieved the paperwork left on the sideboard. She examined the stove, realizing it was a wood burning unit. "Another expense." While her grandmother might be able to cook on such a stove, she could not. Hell, she didn't have the wherewithal to make food in the microwave. Destiny would be leaving for home at the end of the summer and taking her cooking skills with her. "Come on, Destiny." They hiked to the hotel, working up a ravenous appetite. They opted to eat in the on-site café. When the food had arrived and both had eaten their fill, Olivia decided to broach a delicate subject.

"Uhm, Destiny?"

"Yes?"

"You really don't have any money at all, do you?"

"What do you mean? Of course I have money."

Livy smiled. "You are very thin, even for a student, and while you've not said as much, I believe the only times you eat are when we dine together. Can you really cook?"

The student bristled. "Yes, I can cook."

Olivia thought she may have stepped over the line until she saw the sag of her lunch mate's shoulders.

"You have discovered my secret." She sighed. "I had just enough money to get here. I figured I would get employment in a fast food restaurant or on a local cruise ship. I'd get my meals as a bonus. Then we bumped into each other and things took a different tack. I'm sorry for the subterfuge." She slumped into the chair.

Olivia offered a smile. "Don't worry. I had to work to get my degree too. Well, now begs the question of, can you cook and bake on a wood stove?"

Destiny brightened. "Oh, yes. My mum was from a small village in her country. They still used that type of unit. When she came to England, it was all she knew. They didn't have a lot of money, so they let a small house in a village outside Oxford. It was very similar to the one where she lived in the old country. I learned to cook on one."

"Well, we'll just have to secure a cord of wood, some kindling, and make sure you have plenty of matches." Livy's phone trilled and she answered. A smile blossomed and she sat up in the chair. "Of course. Tomorrow? Great." She grinned at Destiny. "My belongings will be in port tomorrow. I'll have to contact my cousin about getting a moving van to bring them to the house. This will solve the issue of a table, chairs and so many other items.

"I guess you will be protecting more than just the house, now. I'd like to go back and do some basic cleaning. I can try to get rid of a few more decades of dust before my household arrives."

Destiny stood. "Let's get going."

Olivia beamed. She stood, peeled off enough bills to pay for lunch and provide the server with a hefty tip. This time, they used the car.

# Chapter Fifteen

Rafaele opened the office in his home, plunking his briefcase on the desk. He grabbed a blank manila folder and marked the address on the upper tab, sliding the signed contracts inside. Sitting in his comfortable, old chair, he unlocked the drawer and pulled out the monthly reports given to him by Genisse. He reached into his briefcase and pulled the stack of the same reports he'd just retrieved from the bank. The size difference was shocking. He would need to go through each month. The prospect gave him indigestion.

His desk phone rang. Automatically, he picked it up. *"Pronto?"*

"Raffy. What's up?"

It was Paolo; the last person he wanted to speak with at the moment.

"Did you get the contract with that snooty American?"

"I'm still working on it. What do you need, Paolo?"

"I just wanted to check and see if you had any work for me. I'm going to need cash pretty soon."

"Like I told Genisse to relay to you, when I have work, I'll call. Can't you borrow from one of your lady friends?"

"Things are a little dry right now. Seems husbands and boyfriends can only be lied to for so long before they get wise…and angry."

"So, I've heard. Since I have a mountain of paperwork to do, I'll talk to you later. *Ciao.*"

*"Ciao,* Raffy."

Rafaele couldn't quite put his finger on what it was about his conversation with Paolo, but his old friend seemed—guarded. He'd heard through the rumor grapevine his *amico* was driving a brand-new Fiat Spider. Raffy knew he wasn't paying him enough to afford that kind of vehicle. A 500C maybe; not a Spider. In the last couple years, Paolo had pulled away from him and effected a more reclusive nature. Oh, sure, he was jovial at work, but the boys' nights they used to share no longer happened. Finally, the truth dawned on him. It hadn't been just the last few years. Paolo had been pulling away since he'd returned from University. He really was angry at Rafaele for choosing to take his father's offer of education over their friendship, as Paolo saw it.

"I may choose to spend my life in Ollolai, but on my terms." He pushed back in the chair. It was too bad his nonna had passed away this last winter. He could really use her advice. In the meantime, he'd attempt to make some sense of the pile of reports from the bank.

~ * ~

Olivia had perused the contract between herself and R & P Construction. It was no different than one from the US. There were more restrictions laid down by the local government agencies, but for the most part, it was a contract to make repairs to a home she owned. The timeline was set to have all the work completed and inspected with passing marks in three years.

The more she thought about it, the more she decided she wanted a Romeo balcony and a skylight. Since she was funding this adventure, Mr. Sonna could just get over his objections and make it happen. She stretched in the bed, having dropped in around 9:00 pm last night. She wasn't particularly a night owl, and nine o'clock was early, even for her, but she and Destiny had morphed into cleaning tornadoes after lunch yesterday. She swore they mopped the floors three times, and they were still pulling up dirt. Maybe in three years, her house would be clean.

Destiny let her know she was at the crux of important research this morning and wouldn't be around until noon. That was fine by Livy. After her phone call from the shipping lines, she'd called her cousin.

*"Ufficio del Sindaco."*

"Angelica?

*"Si."*

"It's Olivia."

"Oh, good afternoon. What can I do for you, *cugina?"*

Olivia smiled. *Guess I'm being accepted.* "My belongings will be here at Cagliari tomorrow. Do you know of a moving company that can bring them to my house?"

*"Si.* Leave this to me. Then maybe you can invite me to dinner for payment, *si?"*

Livy laughed. "As long as my new friend is here, *si.* I don't really know how to cook."

There was a noise at the other end of the phone. *Sounds like tsking.* "When she leaves, I will teach you myself. Every woman should know how to cook. If not for someone, just for herself!"

"Then I accept your offer. Will you call and let me know when to expect things to arrive?"

*"Naturalmente. Ciao."*

*"Ciao."*

A short time later, Olivia's cell rang, and Angelica announced two good pieces of news.

"The moving company is another *cugino* you will meet tomorrow around three o'clock. The people with the electric company said they would be at the house *around* noon. If they are not there by the time the movers arrive, call me. I will give them a piece of my mind in a language they can understand."

Olivia laughed. "I will. *Grazie,* Angelica, *mil grazie."*

"Anything for *famiglia."*

So here sat Livy on her front step—yet again. She realized she was still thinking in business mode. Since she had nothing but time, however long or short it took, would make little difference.

She made her way to the back of the house and looked over the area enclosed in a simple split wood railing fence. There were a few trees and bushes scattered among the boulders. A flash of sparkle pierced her right eye. She followed the light to a large rock and bent to investigate. A small cross with a red center stone lie at the foot of the stone. She picked up the delicate jewelry and turned it over. On the back in a small intricate hand, the initials FP were carved. *Could this really be?* Nonna once mentioned, in passing, that the only piece of personal jewelry she'd taken had been lost between the house and the road where she'd caught the bus to Cagliari.

Olivia held the cross to her heart. She would put it on and never take it off. A crunching sound in front of the house distracted her treasure hunt. She trotted around the side to see Rafaele's truck making its way up the drive. Once parked, he exited and moved toward her.

*"Buon giorno, signorina."*

*"Buon giorno, signor."*

"I received a call from Angelica asking me to arrive a bit early. She wants to have a native speaker here to intercede, if needed."

Olivia lifted a brow. *"Grazie.* I think I can handle this." She continued to look into his warm brown eyes and noted the tiny lines at the corner. *Hopefully, from laughing.* "I'll feel more confident knowing there is someone here who will tell me the truth of what is being said."

Shaking hands, they entered the house. They'd not been inside but ten minutes when a delivery truck arrived. Rafaele recognized the truck from Salvatore's store. "These will be supplies for working on the house. Is there someplace we can put them?"

Livy took his hand and led him to the back of the house, pointing out the lean-to. "Will that work?"

*"Perfetto. Grazie."*

"With Destiny here at night, there will be someone to keep an eye on things."

"Oh, that's not really necessary but I know it will make you feel better."

Rafaele dashed to the front and directed the driver up the narrow path to the shed. After several trips, the two men shook hands. The driver took off to be replaced by the moving van.

"Looks as if today is going to be busy." Rafaele nodded to the incoming van.

Olivia turned to watch the mid-size delivery van rumble up the drive. "I sure hope so. I want to start living in my house. I enjoy the hotel, but it's not really home."

Rafaele agreed. The driver of the van automatically approached Rafaele to ask where he wanted the items.

Olivia watched as Rafaele told him the delivery was for the young lady.

The guy turned to her and gave her the once over. He broke into a smirk. *"Italiano?"*

She caught a quick glance from Raffy who smirked. Olivia decided to play the dumb American. *"Un po."* She saw the wheels turn in the driver's eyes.

He turned to Rafaele and spoke in the local dialect. "This is a really small load; kitchen table and chairs, a few living room items, and a bedroom suite. There are some boxes of other things, but I believe I can make this stretch out for a couple days." He winked and jauntily headed to the truck. He maneuvered the vehicle to put the ramp on the top step and roll the large items directly into the house. When he exited his side, the passenger door opened and a thin, reedy young man jumped out. The pair conferred, returning to the back of the van to open it up.

As they started, Livy moved next to Rafaele. "When would you like to tell him I understand Sardinian quite well?"

Raffy scratched his day's growth. "Right after they take your bed to the master bedroom and set it up. Why don't I ask him to do that first saying you'll want to sleep there tonight?"

Olivia smiled. "Okay." She wandered to the kitchen area to wait for the electric company men while the movers put her furniture in the house.

Rafaele ambled to the van. "Gentlemen. The lady of the house asked if you would get the bedroom furniture to the master suite on the second floor. She wishes to stay in her home this evening."

The men traded grimaces. "Of course." They found the frame for the queen-sized bed and each grabbed one side. Rafaele directed them to the room where the furniture was to be set. During the hour it took for the pair to move the bedroom suite in, the electric company workers had come, turned on the juice, and left. Raffy had made quick work of the visit and went to locate the movers, finding them inside their van smoking.

"Gentlemen. The lady prefers you not smoke in her house." He started to walk away catching them rolling their eyes. "Oh, yes. I wanted to let you know, while Signorina Martin speaks minimal Italian, she is fluent in Sardinian." He watched the driver's cigarette stop mid-way to his mouth.

"So, she…"

"Yes. She understood what you said to me. I would suggest you unload her items with as much care and speed as possible and be on your way. One more thing…she is a Porcu." He watched the men stub out their cigarettes in the vehicle's ashtray and bolt to the back. The rest of the furniture and boxes were unloaded within two and a half hours.

Olivia was impressed. "What did you say to them? I can't say I've seen American movers get done that fast."

Rafaele shrugged his shoulders. "I told them you wished for them not to smoke on your property, that you were fluent in Sardinian, and, this was the catalyst, you are a Porcu."

"Is Nonna's family really that connected?"

Raffy looked at the hazel eyes searching his face. "Yes. It would take a few hours to explain how and why but know the Porcu's are very important to this community, to this island."

"Wow. You have your furniture."

"AHH!" Olivia whipped around to face Destiny. "Where'd you come from? I didn't hear you."

"Uhm, the field?"

Livy was clutching her chest. "You scared the daylights out of me. Yes, I have my furniture. I'll need to go to the hotel and collect my stuff from there then check out. I suspect a trip to the grocer will be in order."

"The refrigerator works?" Destiny walked up the steps toward the

74

house.

Olivia stopped. "I don't know. Guess we need to find out." She followed Destiny into the kitchen. They wiggled the old box away from the wall, groaning at the collection of items stashed behind it by some small furry creature.

"We know what we'll be doing tomorrow." Destiny groaned.

"Yep."

Locating a plug and socket that looked as if it should be in the Smithsonian Institute, Olivia connected the two. There was a sigh, cough producing a puff of dirt, then the old machine began humming. The girls looked at each other and smiled.

"We have refrigeration." Olivia said.

"Guess a trip to the grocer is in order," Destiny replied.

"Did you see it on your way through town?"

"No, I wasn't really paying attention to that when I came through. Maybe we should ask Rafaele?"

They dashed out the front door to see the cloud of dirt behind the truck exiting the driveway to the road.

"Darn it. I guess we'll just have to go to town and do a short tour. I'm sure it won't take us long to find the grocery. If we can't, I'll just visit my cousin again. You know, she's probably going to put me to work if I keep showing up at her doorstep."

Destiny giggled. "Would that be so bad?"

Olivia thought for a moment. "No. Not really."

# Chapter Sixteen

The move in was relatively smooth. The ensuing renovation…a nightmare. Destiny was close to asking for another dream weaver to finish this assignment. Olivia and Rafaele argued about *everything.* She swore they did it just to aggravate each other. The result, however, was making her doubt her ability to keep her cool under fire.

"All you need to do is cut a small hole in the ceiling and…" Olivia pointed to a spot near the joist.

"You don't just cut small holes near a joist. It's a bearing beam; just like the wall over there," he pointed to the window where she'd wanted a balcony, "and the wall in the kitchen and…"

*"BASTA!"*

Olivia and Rafaele jumped. The shouted command echoed around the nearly empty house.

"You two will follow me. NOW!"

Looking at each other in surprise, they trailed behind Destiny into the kitchen.

"Sit." She pointed to the table and chairs. Olivia took one side of the table, Raffy the other, crossing his arms in defiance.

"Every single day, you two find a way to disagree on—something."

"How can you know? You're out doing your archeology study." Olivia frowned.

"I have my ways. You will get along while I'm here, so I don't have to worry when I leave the house. Olivia, what do you know about Rafaele?"

"I know what I need to. He's a licensed contractor that was

recommended by my cousin."

"Uh-huh. Rafaele, what did Olivia do in America before she moved here?"

He shrugged. "I don't need to know the history of my clients. I just need to do the work in their home and get paid."

"Fine. But how is that happening here? All I see and hear is arguing. You two will not move a muscle until you discover a bit of personal history about each other, starting now. First question will be; did you go to university and, if so, what did you study? The next question will have to do with family." She glared at the pair. "Get started." She turned and disappeared under the stairwell.

Rafaele cocked his head slightly. "Did you go to university?"

Olivia nodded.

"What did you study?"

"Finance."

Rafaele uncrossed his arms. "Finance?"

She nodded again.

"So you can do auditing?"

Olivia indicated she could. "Yes. That is part of the finance program, but my specialty was stocks. I was a stockbroker."

"Wow. I would never have guessed."

"Most people don't. Your turn. Did you go to university?"

"Yes."

"Did you get a degree and in what?"

"I got my bachelor's in Engineering…civil engineering."

It was Olivia's turn to be floored. "An engineer. I would have thought there were dozens of jobs in the big cities. Why did you come to Ollolai?"

Rafaele shifted in his seat. "My father wanted me to have an education, so being a dutiful son, I went to college to study. What I really wanted to do was work on my uncle's sheep farm and stay on the island. I was glad to have the opportunity to attend university. I took a job in Italy, Rome to be exact, and hated every minute of it. I guess I'm just a small island person. I missed the quiet at night and knowing the people in the restaurant when you go out to eat. I hated the traffic and pollution. So, when my nonna became ill, it was a good excuse to move back to Ollolai."

Olivia had been worrying her lip between her teeth. "I owe you an apology. I was judging you by your job."

Rafaele graced her with a rare smile. "I, too, am guilty of such an act. Shall we begin once more?"

She smiled. "I'd like that."

They sat and talked for an hour, sharing family stories and life experiences. When Rafaele felt comfortable, he broached a subject he was unsure of.

"Ms. Martin."

Olivia's eyebrows rose. "So formal. What do you want?"

He cleared his throat and shifted in the chair. "I have a situation which makes me very distressed."

Olivia nodded. She could see whatever it was that Rafaele needed made him very uncomfortable. "Rafaele?"

"*Si.*"

"Why don't you just say what the situation is and don't worry about me judging you?"

He sighed and clasped his hands together. Pulling in a deep breath, he started. "I went to the supply store to order for this job. I've been working with them since I came back to Ollolai. But the owner informed me I could no longer put my supplies on account."

"Oh."

"This has never happened. I pay my bills and don't abuse the privilege, so I'm very confused. Would you audit my books to see if there is a—problem—I don't know about? I asked Cecilia at the bank to provide me with the account history. When she came back with it, I was floored. What I receive from my secretary at the office is but a page long. The bank provided nearly three times the papers."

"Will this affect the work here?"

"No. I am a professional. I will do my best work no matter the outcome."

"Okay. Bring the papers tomorrow and I'll get started."

*"Grazie."* He reached across the table and grasped her hands in his.

His touch sent an electric current blazing up her arm. She looked into his brown eyes and felt the flutter of her heart. *Oh, no. I can't let this happen again.*

*"Prego.* No promises."

Raffy pulled his hand back and held one up. "No promises. I understand. I need to continue the work upstairs. I will investigate putting in a skylight and attaching a balcony. But..." he smiled at her, "...no promises."

"Fair enough."

Destiny watched the scene with growing hope. *This is how it is supposed to be.*

# Chapter Seventeen

Olivia spread the papers across the tabletop. There was no way she could immediately see how his secretary was finding the numbers she gave to him. From her quick perusal of the accounts, there was a great deal of money not accounted for in Rafaele's monthly reports.

She tracked more money going out than coming in, creating a loss. How could Rafaele be solvent with so much missing? She would need to ask him the following day when he came to put finishing touches on the master bedroom. They had sat down and discussed her "want" list, coming to an agreement on the two items she had desired. He'd been very patient and explained why the skylight would be more of a burden than a delight. Seems if it was installed when the building was put up the first time, accommodations were made to ensure the window was sealed tight. Afterward, there was always the chance of leakage of both moisture and heat.

Olivia agreed the idea was just a fancy, but she was adamant about having a small balcony off the master bedroom. She and Rafaele had batted the particulars back and forth for a week or so until Destiny put a halt to their bickering.

They sat at the kitchen table, this time with coffee, and went over the idea and construction for installation of the balcony. Livy compromised on the size, and Rafaele agreed to install the additional tier. Olivia was happy, Rafaele was happy, and Destiny was happy.

~ * ~

The knock on the front door was subtle. Olivia knew immediately it was Raffy. "Come in, *signore. Buon giorno.*"

*"Buon giorno, signorina.* How are you this morning?"

"I'm doing very well. Come. Sit and have coffee before you go to work. I need to speak with you for a moment."

A worried look crossed Rafaele's face. "I hope it's not bad news."

Livy poured coffee made from a new cappuccino machine she'd bought herself as a housewarming gift. "Maybe yes, maybe no."

As he picked up the coffee and took a sip, he smiled. "This is *molto bene.*"

"Thank you. What do you do when the bank or the store says there isn't enough money to cover a bill?"

Rafaele sputtered. "That is a bit personal, don't you think?"

Olivia sipped her brew. "You asked me to find out about your account. Unfortunately, knowing this information is important to the direction I need to take."

Silence descended on the pair. Rafaele twisted in his chair. "I cover it with my own money."

Olivia's eyebrows rose. "Okay. I won't ask."

Raffy quickly recovered. "It is not what you think. I still take on projects for the mainland and receive payment from the large companies who employ me."

"So you do this…"

"… because I want to."

"I'm sorry. It was a necessary piece of information. I have to go to the store to buy a toaster. You are on your own. If you leave before I get back, please put the key in the niche outside."

"Of course."

~ * ~

Rafaele took his cup with him and headed to the second floor.

Despite the small hiccups, the job had been easily accomplished. Besides, the more time he spent with Olivia, the more he liked it. He was becoming quite fond of this American transplant. Maybe when the job was completed, he would ask her out. *No.* That was Paolo's style, not his. The thought of his friend brought a stab of pain to him. He'd not seen nor heard from the man since the day they'd been granted the job. What could be so important he wouldn't even call? Rafaele would find out; after the job was over.

~ * ~

Olivia loved going into the stores in Ollolai. They were different than those in Portland; more homey. She was standing in front of the toaster display when the bell at the front door rang.

"Salvatore!"

Shuffling from the back brought the owner to the counter. "Paolo. What can I do for you?"

"I need you to return these electrical supplies. They aren't quite right. The house is so old, and the wiring is turning into a pain to upgrade."

"No can do, Paolo."

"Why not? You did it last time."

"Since you came in last time, Rafaele has changed his purchase policy. He told me no one but he is allowed to buy and return supplies."

Olivia heard a muttered swear word.

"But these are the supplies he purchased. He asked me to return them and get the money."

"I can't. Unless he is standing here with those supplies in his hand asking, no more cash for returned supplies."

This time the swear word was loud and vulgar, followed by the slamming of the door and jangling of the bell. Olivia decided she would get a toaster later. She moved to the store window and watched as a flashy Fiat Spider smoked the tires down the street. This was a situation where Rafaele would have to do the investigation.

She drove the car into the driveway and parked. The carport was a project that would be put on the back burner. At the end of this week, she was to turn in the rental. Afterward, she wasn't sure what she would do. First things first. Entering the house, she put her purse on the sideboard and took a deep breath. Walking up the steps to the second floor, she wasn't quite sure how to present her suspicions to Rafaele. Paolo was the man's best friend. Most men would believe their friends over any woman.

She pushed open the door and watched in awe as Raffy put finishing touches on the balcony railing. "Thank you. I will enjoy every moment I spend out there."

Rafaele smiled. "Just don't go out for at least one day. The paint needs to dry." He set his paint brush on the rim of the paint bucket and wiped his hands on a rag. "What brings you up here now?"

Olivia looked at the floor then into his eyes. "I think I know what has been happening to your business account, but you'll need to put the final piece to this puzzle."

"Can't you give me a clue?"

"I would rather you come to your own conclusion. If I'm wrong and tell you what I think, our friendship will fall apart. I don't want that to happen."

"What is it you need me to do?"

"You need to ask the storekeeper for his records on your purchases and returns for the last year. I believe you will have your answer. If it is what I think, you may not like the resolution."

"That may be, but I have to know what is happening to my company. I'll talk to Salvatore tomorrow."

"Salvatore? Like the mayor?" Olivia was surprised.

Rafaele chuckled. "Yes. This is a very small community and we cannot afford to have a paid mayor. Salvatore gets a small salary and the honor of casting the deciding vote on town issues."

"Hmm. Not sure I would want that responsibility."

"I told them no when they asked me to run."

Olivia burst out laughing. "Smart move." She turned to leave then stopped and faced Rafaele. "Will I see you tomorrow?"

A sly grin began to creep over his face. "Try and stop me. I'll get the paperwork from Salvatore and we can go over it together. No arguing."

She nodded. "Right. I really don't want Destiny yelling again. I thought the English had good manners. That woman could out yell a drunken football player."

Rafaele laughed. *"Domani."*

Olivia impulsively blew him a kiss, blushing after having done so. He smiled and returned the gesture.

~ * ~

Rafaele walked into the shop, the bell announcing his arrival. "Salvatore!"

*"Si.* Hold your britches. Oh, *signore Sonna. Come stai?"*

*"Buono.* I would like to have copies of all the paperwork from my account for the last year."

"A year? I send all this to Genisse. Why do you need it?"

*"Per favore."*

"Okay, okay. It might take a minute or two. I have to ask the missus to make the copies. She's going to want to go out to dinner for this."

Rafaele smiled. Yes, that would indeed be Aurora. "Tell her *grazie."*

"Yeah, yeah." Salvatore mumbled into the back area of the store. He came back out behind the counter. "I'm sorry the electrical items didn't work for you. If you bring them to me, I can find replacements."

"What are you talking about?" Rafaele stiffened.

"Paolo came in yesterday and wanted to return a bucketful of electrical plugs and sockets for cash. Didn't you send him?"

Raffy's jaw muscles tightened. He finally said, "Not that I recall. Maybe I told him before we spoke."

Salvatore opened his mouth to reply but his wife hollered.

*"E fatto."*

"Excuse me." He retrieved the paperwork and delivered it to

84

Rafaele. "Here you go. See you soon?"

"*Si, caio.*"

"*Caio.*"

Rafaele was tempted to search through the records but the way he was feeling would not make it safe for him to drive should he do so. He took his truck straight to Olivia's. He knocked then entered, finding her at the kitchen table with paperwork in neat piles.

"Good morning."

She looked up. "Oh, this isn't good. You spoke to me in English. What's going on, Rafaele?"

He put the stack in front of her. "I would like us to go through this together."

"Coffee?"

"Do you have anything stronger?"

Olivia looked at the tense expression on his face and opted not to mention it was only ten in the morning. "I think so."

She found a small bottle of whiskey and set it in front of him. "Whiskey. Not sure of the quality, but probably has a hefty kick."

"Thank you." He opened the small bottle and drained the contents. "I think I know what you might have witnessed yesterday."

"Oh?"

"Yes. Salvatore mentioned a visit by Paolo to the store to return merchandise for cash. Right?"

Livy sighed. It was difficult to let someone know they'd been betrayed. She was a first-hand witness to the feelings of anger. "Yes. But let's go through the account ledger to see if maybe this was just a one-time happening. Maybe he was running low on funds. There could be many explanations."

Rafaele humphed.

The audit took three hours of finding, cross referencing, and double checking to come to the conclusion Olivia had hoped wouldn't be. Rafaele's best friend was stealing from him to the tune of hundreds of thousands of dollars. It had been happening since he'd first opened the company.

"I hate to believe this, but the proof is in black and white. Tell me, did you see him leave in a vehicle?" Rafaele looked up from the mass of papers.

Olivia pulled in a breath. "Yes. A new Fiat Spider. He burned rubber all the way down the street."

Raffy frowned. "Burned rubber?"

"Yes. Spun the tires so much there was smoke." Olivia said.

"Ah, yes. That would be a Paolo action."

"What are you going to do, Raffy?" Livy's forehead corrugated in concern.

"I'm not sure. I must think about this. May I come by tomorrow?"

"Of course." Olivia walked him to the door and watched him leave. Her heart hurt for him.

"Is everything okay?" Destiny appeared at Livy's elbow.

"No. Rafaele just discovered his best friend has been stealing large amounts of money from him for a very long time." She went to the sink and rinsed out the cups they had been using.

"Would you like me to fix lunch?"

"Thanks, Destiny. I really don't have an appetite. Say, when are you leaving for school?"

Destiny stopped and turned to answer Olivia. "I have about two days of wor…research to do then I'll be leaving here. I meant to say something but have been so busy putting together my paper."

Olivia looked stricken. "Two days? Are you sure you can't stay? You really are the only friend I have here."

"I don't think that's true. You have Rafaele and your cousin. You'll find others who will help you to fit into the community."

"Maybe so. First, Taylor; now, you. I'm beginning to wonder if I made the right decision."

Destiny moved to her side and ran a hand across her back. "You did. I can tell, you did."

# Chapter Eighteen

Destiny finished tying the knots of the tapestry. It was really quite beautiful. She rolled it up and set it aside. "Now to the other." The second weaving had hit her with such force, she'd fought a headache for a week. The background was quite unusual. There were stars but she didn't recognize any of the constellations.

In the middle was a town, but it appeared to be deserted except for the two people looking up at the buildings and several dogs peeking around corners. She didn't understand it, but she was not going to question her assignments.

Putting the smaller tapestry into her knapsack, she tucked the Ollolai one under her arm and headed to the stairs. At the foot of the stairs, she turned and bid the loom goodbye.

"You have given me such pleasure. I hope our Miss Olivia chooses to learn to weave and takes the opportunity to work with you. Goodbye, friend."

She climbed the stairs and closed the door for the last time. Rounding the corner, she stopped and stepped back. Olivia and Rafaele were entangled in a very serious kiss. This was exactly what she had been sent to do. She cleared her throat.

She heard the shuffle of feet and came around the corner. "Hello. Rafaele. I'm so glad you are here. I have finished my gift and wanted you both to see it." She unfurled the tapestry and listened as the pair inhaled surprise. The picture showed the house, plants growing, garage built, and a couple bicycles in the drive. A man and woman stood on the porch arm in arm looking very happy. Two little ones were chasing each other.

"I have enjoyed my time here, but I must go. Please take care of each other." She moved to Olivia and gave her a hug. She shook Rafaele's hand. Opening the door, she hiked out the front and to the street. She wasn't worried about transportation. There always seemed to be a vehicle to get her to her destination. The only thing she knew about the new destination was there were many unoccupied buildings and the stars played into this story. Oh, there were also a few people and lots of dogs. She whistled as she moved toward the main road. Another assignment then vacation.

~ * ~

Rafaele pulled Olivia into his arms. "Tell me, how did you meet your friend, Destiny?"

She shrugged her shoulders. "She just sort of showed up here a day or so after I arrived."

"Really?"

"Yes. Why?"

"I happened to be at one of the sites she was supposed to be working, on the day she was to be there. The place was empty."

"Raffy. Don't be so cynical. Maybe she went somewhere else."

"I don't think so. Do you remember her telling us she knew when we were fighting? Even if she wasn't here?"

"Yes, so?"

"Come look." He took her hand and let her to the tapestry. He pointed to some areas at the bottom of the weaving. "These spots here have been...repaired."

"She made a few mistakes. She did say she was a novice."

He looked at her and smiled. "Does this really look as if a novice has woven this? I don't think so. I think your friend, Destiny, is exactly what her names implies."

Olivia exploded in a laugh. "Oh, Raffy. Don't be superstitious. All the stories about the fates, and destiny, and those types of things are myths.

None of them are real."

He smirked. "If you say so."

"I hate to change the subject, but what are you going to do about Paolo?"

"Nothing."

"WHAT?"

He crossed his arms over his chest. "Nothing. I called Genisse into the office yesterday and presented her with all the evidence of their thievery. She broke down and told me the story. Paolo has a gambling habit he has been feeding with my money. He promised to take Genisse away from here and her abusive husband, but that never came to fruition. When he went out and bought the Fiat Spider, she knew she had to extricate herself from the situation or be taken down with him.

"I never gave him any financial information like the bank number or passwords to accounts or computers. He wasn't interested. It may just have saved my hide. Genisse will be dealing with her husband, a rather nasty character, so I don't see the point of adding to her misery.

"Paolo has the gambling syndicate to answer to, and they don't take lightly to people who rip them off. Personally, I don't think anything I could do would be anywhere near as punishing as what the syndicate will do."

Olivia thought about what he'd said. "You're right."

Rafaele raised an eyebrow. "Can I mark that on the calendar?"

"What?"

"You said I was right."

"Go ahead. I'll just tell people you had too much wine and heard me wrong."

He laughed. "And they would believe you. May I take you to lunch, *Signorina?*"

Olivia smiled. "Lead the way."

# Other books by Christie L. Kraemer
## Available at Rogue Phoenix Press

## *Healthy Homicide*

Two murders have occurred at the Barrel Springs Day Spa. Police hurry to find the method and reason before anyone else is murdered.

MANIC READER REVIEWS says: Healthy Homicide by C.L. Kraemer is an intriguing plot driven mystery. The plot is well written and pretty much carries the whole story...

## *Dragons Among Us*

In a world full of anomalies such as the platypus and self reproducing Komodo dragon, is the human race willing to accept that dragons may be real?

Sapien Draconi-human-dragon shape shifters-all over the world face this dilemma every day. The question has become life and death as their species is plagued with unexpected and unwanted shifting in the most unlikely of places.

The Ancient Ones-full-blooded dragons-can offer advice, but few seem to put forward workable solutions to the problem.

The fate of the shape shifters hangs in the balance, and an answer must be found before the Homo Sapiens find, dissect, and hunt Sapien Draconi to extinction.

## Dragons Among The Eagles

Aleda Sable faces the toughest decision of her life--to stay in dragon form, live as a two-legged or put one foot in the human world and one talon in the dragon world.

An urgent call from her newspaper editor sends Aleda to report on an accident whose driver appears to be a dragon. Authorities have the scene locked down and aren't allowing access to anyone. Television broadcasts flash pictures of scaly legs hanging from a crashed car. However, the bodies disappear into thin air. When the stations try follow-up reports, all they find are state highway workers busily tearing up the roads.

In determining the truth of the shifter disappearances, Aleda finds the truth of her own dilemma.

## Shattered Tomorrows

Lucy Daniels has a secret--a deeply guarded secret.

Her life was going along just fine until she accompanied her best friend, Cassie, to her attorney's suite on top of the Equitable Building in downtown Salem, Oregon.

Once inside the lawyer's office, the world turned upside down and Lucy was forced to face a demon from her past. Thirty years ago, life had been different. Lucy had discovered Prince Charming and was headed to her happily ever after.

That's when the devil intervened and because of her brush with the devil, innocent people died.

## Joker's Wild

Four brothers raised in the Northwest.

Two choose to stay and pursue life in Oregon. Two are seduced by the promise of Hollywood.

Life throws the Palmer brothers an ugly curve when two are killed in preventable accidents. Even more upsetting is the lack of justice in the trials of the perpetrators.

The remaining brothers will find justice using a shared passion of all the participants--motorcycle poker runs.

# C. L. Kraemer
is also featured in these anthologies available at
Rogue Phoenix Press

## *A Different Kind of Valentine*

A collection of four short stories:

### *Witness* by k. J. Dahlen

When Colten finds an injured woman the police are looking for her, should he trust his own judgement about keeping her hidden from the law even if it means she might kill him?

### *The Prize* by C. L. Kraemer

A computer geek learns valuable life lessons when he is given his dream car as well as a condo and the perfect job.

### *Crazy 'bout You* by Clay Renick

Can a psychologist and a romance writer find true love in time for Valentines                                                                  Day?

### *Time Changes* by Nicolette Zamora

Laurie is just about ready to give up on love when she spies Rob Hender, her high school sweethearts older brother.

## *A St. Patrick's Day Tale*
by
Christine Young, C. L. Kraemer, Genene Valleau

Tumble through time…

…to Ireland in 1817, when tensions are high between Protestants and Chatolics and faey people guide the fate of villagers. A lovely Catholic lass stumbles upon the weakly ritual fisticuffing between Irish lads. She falls into the lap of a handsome young Protestant. Family ties, grudges, and two conniving faeries threaten their budding love. But the faeries outsmart themselves when they hijack a time machine that has mysteriously appeared in their forest and are whisked to…

…Eugene, Oregon in the 20$^{th}$ century, amid a property feud between the local faeries and night elves. The conniving faeries from Olde Ireland try to stir up more mischief. However, a warrior gnome convinces the magic folk to control their own destiny, and forces the intruding faeries to take refuge in the time machine again, spinning their way toward…

…A modern day castle in western Oregon. An eccentric inventor is determined to reclaim his wayward time machine and save his beloved wife from her latest misadventure. If only they can travel safely past the black hole…

## *A Valentine's Anthology*

*The Lending Library*-a fantasy by C. L. Kraemer

Faeries try to fit into the human world when the forest where they make their home is destroyed by a mysterious enemy.

*Chasing Rainbows*-a contemporary romance by Genene Valleau

An eccentric aunt, an inventive uncle, a mother who wears poodle skirts, and a brother who wears pearls provide a hilarious backdrop for the courtship of a young woman who yearns for a "normal" family.

*The Gift*-an historical romance by Christine Young

A man and a woman on opposite sides of the Civil War get a second chance at love after one final battle returns soldiers to their war-torn homes to rebuild their lives.

*VISIT OUR WEBSITE*
*FOR THE FULL INVENTORY*
*OF QUALITY BOOKS*:
*http://www.roguephoenixpress.com*

# Rogue Phoenix Press

*Representing Excellence in Publishing*

*Quality trade paperbacks and downloads*

*in multiple formats,*

*in genres ranging from historical to contemporary romance, mystery and science fiction.*

*Visit the website then bookmark it.*

*We add new titles each month*

www.ingramcontent.com/pod-product-compliance
Lightning Source LLC
Chambersburg PA
CBHW070639130626
46555CB00006B/2619